FIERCE

NINA LEVINE

Dear Rosa,

Nina Levine

xx

DEDICATION

Fierce is dedicated to my family.
Family isn't always those related by blood.
I love you all.

1

SCOTT

I killed the engine of my bike and removed my helmet while I surveyed the argument that was currently occurring between Madison and our father. They both appeared to be past the point of angry and Madison was jabbing her finger at his chest. It was probably time for me to step in so I left my bike and walked towards the front of the clubhouse where they were. Madison had her back to me so she didn't see me coming but Dad did and lifted his chin at me.

"Scott." He greeted me, minus a smile.

Madison stopped mid sentence and whipped her head around, her angry eyes narrowing as they landed on me. "Where's J? I thought he was with you," she said.

"He's at Indigo sorting out some problems. What's going on with you two?"

She scowled and went to answer me but Dad cut in.

"I've asked Madison to come over for dinner tonight but she has refused. With J getting back yesterday, I thought it would be a good time for us all to get together and start to work through this bullshit mess we are in. You should come too." Rather than sounding angry, he just appeared resigned.

"You created this bullshit mess," I reminded him, "The day you decided not to keep your dick in your pants. And the day you decided to hit your wife. Don't fuckin' expect us to forget either of those anytime soon." I could feel my anger levels rising but fought to remain calm. He wasn't worth it.

Madison visibly relaxed and the scowl was wiped off her face. She turned back to Dad. "We won't be there tonight," she said, quieter now, less angry. And then she said to me, "Can we talk when you get some time?"

I nodded. "Sure, I've just got some information to share with Dad and then I'll come find you. You're waiting here for J?"

"Yeah. Thanks," she replied and with one last look at Dad, she pushed through the front door and left us alone outside.

Dad stared after her for a moment, lost in thought, before addressing me, "I've made some bad decisions in my life and I'm fucking paying for them, but this shit with our family needs to be sorted. Your mother wants it dealt with."

I shook my head. "Not gonna happen. And don't

play the Mum card. Jesus." I ran my fingers through my hair and felt the beginning of a headache. Fuck, I needed a drink, or better yet, some pussy to ease it. Yeah, pussy always helped.

He contemplated what I'd said and then nodded tightly. "What do you need to tell me?"

I was over-fucking-joyed that he was moving on and not starting an argument. "Darrell quit so we need a new manager for Indigo. J's there now sorting out staff for the next few days but until we find someone new, J and I will keep it running." This strip club was giving us no end of problems lately.

"Good. Find someone soon though because we need you both for other stuff."

"Yeah, I heard. Bullet's giving you some grief over Blade's crew?" I'd heard this from Griff who kept me in the loop these days because I'd been distancing myself from Dad.

"Christ, it's never fucking ending. Blade's ramped up his supply business, stepping on Bullet's territory. Black Deeds want me to get Blade to back off. Coke is their main game and he's taking from them. Just cause he's my son doesn't mean he's going to listen to me. It's another thing I don't need to be dealing with at the moment. So, yeah, I need you around in case shit goes down."

"I'm not getting involved with Blade. But if it blows back on Storm, I'm on it."

"Well stick close cause I reckon shit's gonna go

down at some point. And think on what I said about our family. It's not just your mother who wants it healed," he muttered before walking away.

I watched him as he got on his bike and took off, and wondered where he was spending his time these days. It was three o'clock in the afternoon and I doubted he was heading home. Neither Madison nor I knew if he was still carrying on with Blade's mother because neither of us had spent any time with him in the last four months.

My phone rang, interrupting my thoughts. I reached into my pocket and grabbed it out to see who it was. Lisa. My neighbour's kid. "Darlin', what's wrong?" I answered her without hesitation because she only ever called me when she had a problem. For a twelve year old, she was surprisingly drama free, so I knew if she called, something was going down.

"Scott, Monty's sick," she said, voice trembling.

"What's wrong with him?" Monty was her cat; her faithful companion in her shitty life.

"His face is all puffy, like a chipmunk, and he isn't eating. He's pretty much just sleeping all the time and he looks so sad."

"How long's he been like that, darlin'?"

"For a few days," she admitted quietly.

Christ. "You should have told me straight away. I'll be there soon, okay." Her mother wasn't equipped to deal with shit like this and I thought I'd made it clear to her to always call on me, but she was the kind of kid who hated asking for help.

"Okay. Thanks, Scott," she said and then hung up.

I shoved my phone back in my pocket and entered the clubhouse, searching for Madison. I'd see what she wanted and then head over to pick up the cat and take him to the vet.

Nash ran into me as I rounded the corner to go into the kitchen. "Did you sort Darrell's shit out?" he asked.

"Nope. The fucker quit instead," I answered him.

"He's an asshole so we're better off without him."

He was right but it'd left me screwed because now on top of everything else I had to do for Storm, I also had to run Indigo. "The girls are pleased that he's gone, especially Velvet." She was Indigo's favourite stripper so keeping her happy was on my agenda. Darrell was too fucking handsy with the girls and had put the hard word on most of them. Just because they took their clothes off for a living didn't give him the right to expect a quick fuck out of them whenever he needed his dick wet.

"Good," Nash said.

Something in his tone grabbed my attention. "Why are you so interested in this? Indigo's not your gig." Unless of course you counted him visiting the joint for personal pleasure which he did often.

He shrugged. "Velvet's told me some of the shit that he said and did to her. I didn't like the way he treated them."

I continued to study him. There was something there, something he was keeping close to his chest. "Yeah, we're better off without him but we need a new manager soon, and fucked if I know of one. If you have any ideas let me know."

"Will do," he agreed.

"Okay, I'll catch you later, man. I've got to get a cat to the vet before they close."

"What the fuck? You don't have a cat do you?" he asked.

I shook my head, "Neighbour's cat."

"Michelle's?"

"Yeah. Lisa sounded stressed about it."

"I don't know why you rented your house to that crazy bitch, and sure as hell don't know why you look out for her so much. Not after what she did at Indigo."

"It's not Michelle I care about, brother. She's still a junkie so someone needs to be there for her kid. And she hasn't worked much since we fired her so Lisa goes without a lot."

"And people think you're an asshole," he muttered, and then checked his watch, "Shit, I've gotta go. I'll catch you later."

He headed out of the clubhouse and I went looking for Madison. It didn't take me long to find her; I followed her laughter to the kitchen. It was bloody good to hear her laughing again.

She was chatting with Stoney and grinned at me like

an idiot when she saw me. "Stoney was just telling me how you got drunk last night and - "

I cut her off and glared at Stoney. "Thanks, asshole. You wait your fuckin' turn. Payback's a bitch."

Madison was pissing herself laughing now. "Seriously good shit, Scott. I can't believe you did that!"

"You'd better believe he did that. Our Scotty doesn't discriminate," Stoney threw out there.

"What doesn't he discriminate against?" J asked, entering the room.

I threw up my arms. "Fuck me! I almost went to town on some dick last night. How the fuck was I supposed to know she was a he?"

J, the asshole, started laughing too. "Fuck, man, I feel your pain. I often crave a little cock too, brother. If you feel you need that shit, we won't judge."

I punched him hard in the arm. "Good one, dickhead," I retorted, and then directed at Madison, "What did you want to talk to me about?"

"I just wanted to invite you to a get together at our house on Sunday afternoon," she answered.

J had made his way to Madison and put his arm around her. "Although, there'll be no boys there for you to hook up with so maybe -"

"I'll be there," I muttered and turned to leave. "Everyone's a fuckin' comedian," I threw over my shoulder as I left. I could hear them all laughing as I walked towards the front door. I'd never fucking live it down.

I PULLED up outside my house and saw Lisa looking out for me behind the front curtain next door. It was my house that I rented to her mother and it needed some work. Yesterday I'd noticed that the yard needed mowing, and fuck if I'd ever seen Michelle behind a mower. That was something I always either did or got one of the boys to do. Today I noticed that the windows were caked in a layer of dirt. Another job for the boys.

She let the curtain go and I presumed was on her way outside with Monty. A minute later, I met her at her front gate. She passed me her cat and I noted how bad his face looked. Shit, I wished she'd come to me sooner because he didn't look well. And looking at Lisa, I decided that she didn't look too flash either. Christ, what the fuck was her mother feeding her because, damn, that kid was all skin and bones.

"Thanks, Scott. Mum wouldn't take him to the vet," she admitted reluctantly.

"Yeah, I bet," I said, stopping myself from saying anymore. This kid knew deep in her soul what a crappy fucking hand she'd been dealt, with her mother; she didn't need me pointing it out. "Okay, let's go and get him fixed."

The relief that washed over her face was clear but I

didn't acknowledge it. Lisa didn't like attention and she didn't like people stating the obvious. She was just trying to get through life with as little interruption from others as she could, and I for one, got that. So, I settled her and Monty in my car and we drove to the vet with little conversation passing between us. I think that's why she and I had the kind of relationship that we did; she appreciated my lack of intrusion into her thoughts and I dug her lack of fucking melodramatics.

As we pushed through the door of the vets, she gave me a quick smile. Blink and I'd have missed it, but I didn't. She needed reassurance so I gave it to her; I plastered a smile on my face that could have lit a fucking Christmas tree. And fuck me, she saw it and gave me one back. This kid never smiled. Jesus, someone needed to give her some love.

I took my attention off the kid and directed it to the vet's front desk. My dick jerked when I took in the blonde behind it. Christ, she was a fucking knock out. Long, wavy blonde hair that covered her tits; and they were great tits from what I could tell. Problem was, they were covered up with a white tank top and a shitload of necklaces. And that tank wasn't a low cut one like most of the chicks I met wore, so her assets weren't completely on display. As she continued talking to her customer, I angled my head to try and get a better view. Oblivious to the world while I did this, I missed it when she finished up with him and sent her gaze my way.

"You want me to take it off?" she asked, mild irritation in her voice.

I smirked, "Sure. Go right ahead."

She shook her head and sighed, looking at Lisa. "Because there are children around, I'll refrain from saying what I want to say." Then she turned her attention to the cat, "Oh, poor baby. Pass him here, honey," she said to Lisa who was gripping onto Monty with all her might.

Lisa hesitated, so blondie walked around from behind the counter to come and stand next to her. She knelt down so they were eye to eye, and asked, "What's happened to him?"

Jesus. This chick had my full attention now. Her legs were painted with the tightest jeans I think I'd ever seen someone wear. They rode low on her hips with her tank tucked in. She was rocking the country look with cowgirl boots and a cowgirl looking belt. Actually, she looked like she'd stepped straight out of fucking Nashville.

"Monty got in a fight the other day and now he's sick," Lisa said, in her soft little voice that I could hardly hear. She had her back to me so I couldn't see her eyes, but I bet they were glued to the floor. She had no confidence and that shit me. How could her mother not see that? Not care enough to fucking fix it?

"His face doesn't look too good, does it? If you give him to me I can take him out the back to the vet and we can get him better for you," she said, coaxingly. Yeah, I bet Lisa would hand the cat over now; that voice could charm an alcoholic's last drink from him.

Lisa gave up Monty, and blondie said, "I'll be right back." And with that, she stood and left us as she headed out the back where I guessed the vet was.

I moved to a seat to sit and wait; Lisa followed and sat quietly next to me. She seemed anxious, but then again, she was often like this. Our eyes were drawn to the front door as a guy and his kid came through with their dog. Up until that point we'd been the only ones in the surgery and it was fairly quiet. This guy was talking loudly on his phone, his kid was nagging him about something, trying to get his attention, and his dog was a bundle of energy; suddenly it felt crowded in the tiny waiting room.

He waited at the counter and rung the bell. Blondie didn't come out and the guy was impatient; he hit the bell again. "Harlow!" he bellowed. His kid tugged his shirt repeatedly, muttering shit I didn't understand, and the dog was traipsing around the fucking room because they'd let his leash go. I felt my temper fray at the edges; this guy was a deadset dickhead, and I was biting my tongue for once in my life. For Lisa's sake.

He hit the bell again and then turned to me. "Where the fuck is Harlow?"

I stood up and was about to tell this asshole just what I thought of him when blondie made her way back to the counter.

She smiled at him. Fuck knows why, because he

didn't deserve it. "Rod, sorry to keep you waiting," she said. Her voice was polite but I noticed that it was forced compared to the way she spoke to Lisa before. It was obvious that she knew him and that she didn't really care for him.

"Yeah, well I'm in a fucking hurry, Harlow, so can we move this along? And just for the fucking record, I'm pissed that I had to bring my dog back. You idiots should have taken care of all this last time I was in." he said.

My anger exploded out of me; I couldn't hold it in any longer. "Hey, asshole," I snapped, "Why don't you give her a break? She's busy, and doesn't need dickheads like you speaking to her that way."

His head whipped around and furious eyes landed on me. "This is none of your business so I suggest you stay the fuck out of it."

I stepped into his space, backed him up against the counter, and leant real close. "Now would be the right time for you and your family to leave. I don't like any of the shit that's just gone down, so unless you want trouble between the two of us, leave now," I threatened. When I saw him hesitate, I grabbed a handful of his shirt and snarled, "Did you not understand what I just said, motherfucker?" We glared at each other for a couple of moments before I let him go, shoving him hard against the counter in the process. Keeping my eyes trained on his, I slowly stepped back. Planting my legs wide, I crossed my arms in front of my chest and scowled at him.

Harlow opened her mouth to say something but I caught the movement and flicked my gaze to her for a second, giving her a clear message to stay out of it. She shut her mouth and glared back at me, her eyes widening in a 'what the fuck' type gesture. That shocked the shit out of me, and my concentration was diverted from the asshole to her. I'd never been given that look by a chick before; usually it was J or Nash who challenged me like that. I raised my eyebrows at her, and fuck me if she didn't raise hers right fucking back.

I was snapped out of my distraction when the dickhead decided to listen to me. "Fuck you," he muttered at me, and then jabbed a finger in Harlow's direction, "And your boss will be hearing from me." He grabbed his kid by the arm and his dog by the leash, and made a hasty exit. Not fucking soon enough, as far as I was concerned.

After he left, I looked at Lisa to make sure she was alright. She was looking at me wide eyed but didn't say a word. "You okay?" I asked her.

She nodded. "He wasn't very nice but I feel sorry for his dog; he didn't get to see the vet," she said.

I crouched down in front of her. "No, he wasn't a nice person. There are lots of other vets he can go to though so you don't need to worry about his dog," I said, and waited a moment before saying, "Okay?"

"Okay," she agreed.

I stood back up and turned to Harlow. She was standing with her arms folded across her chest and I struggled not to stare at her tits that were now pushed up by her arms. She had one of the best racks I'd ever seen; a man could die happy after getting an eyeful of that. My dick was in agreement with that. Shit, time to rein this in; there was a kid in the room.

I moved my eyes to hers and was greeted with that irritated look again. "Thanks for that," she said, but I wasn't entirely sure she meant it.

"You'd rather I'd stayed out of it?"

She dropped her arms and slowly shook her head. "Not necessarily, but it was a bit over the top really. I'm used to dealing with assholes like him, so I didn't need you to threaten him like that."

"You shouldn't have to put up with that shit."

She sighed. "No, I shouldn't have to, but that's the general public for you."

"Well, if you have any more trouble from that guy, you call me. I'd be only too fuckin' happy to sort him out for you."

She took me in, and I mean, her eyes raked over me, and assessed me, before she muttered, "I bet you would."

At that moment, we were interrupted by a guy who came from the back room. He looked at me, and asked, "Is Monty your cat?"

Before I could reply, Lisa piped up, "Yes, is he okay?"

Directing his attention to Lisa, he replied, "Well, I need to keep him here overnight because I need to operate on him, but he will be okay. Would you like to come out the back and say goodbye to him?"

Lisa hesitated, looking to me for guidance. "Can I?" she asked me.

I nodded. "Yeah, I'll wait here for you."

She followed the vet, leaving Harlow and I alone. Harlow gave me a strange look and I waited to see what she was going to say. She opened her mouth but then shut it quickly, like she'd thought better of it. Instead, she reached under the counter and produced a sheet of paper. Sliding it, and a pen towards me, she said, "Please fill these details in for Monty. Just make sure you leave us the best number to contact you on in case of an emergency."

"You think something's going to happen to the cat?" I asked. Christ, Lisa would fucking lose it if that cat died.

"He should be okay, but just in case."

"Good, because that kid doesn't need to lose anything else in her life."

Her eyebrows pinched together and she looked confused.

"What?" I asked.

She shook her head. "Nothing."

"Don't give me that bullshit. If you've got something to say, say it."

Her eyes flared with surprise, and then she replied, "Okay, why did you leave it so long to bring Monty in, especially when your daughter obviously loves - "

And then the vet came out, interrupting us again. "Monty needs an operation on his face as he has a cat fight abscess and it's been left too long to be able to treat it with just antibiotics," he said, giving me the look I was sure he reserved for pet owners who didn't look after their pets properly. "We'll call you tomorrow when he's ready to be collected."

I didn't have the time or the fucking inclination to check him on his attitude. "Fine," I said, curtly, and picked up the pen Harlow had given me and filled out their paperwork.

Once I'd filled it out, I slid it back to her and asked, "What time tomorrow do you think it will be? I've got a lot on so it'd be good if you could give me a heads up."

She appraised me, probably noting my shortness with her. I gave zero fucks about what she was thinking. A minute ago, I wanted to rip those jeans off her; now I had no interest in her judgmental ass. Stuck up pussy was my least favourite kind.

"You'll probably be able to collect him anytime after lunch. I'll call you to confirm that," she replied, coolly.

I nodded once, and then said, "Thank you." Turning to Lisa, I asked, "You ready to go, darlin'?"

"Yes." She sounded anything but sure.

"Monty's in the best place tonight. The vet will get him better and then tomorrow we'll come and get him. Yeah?"

"Yeah." That was better; she at least sounded like she believed me.

"Okay, let's go, kiddo," I said, and gently guided her to the front door, giving Harlow one last glance before leaving. It was a shame about her; my hands on her tits would have been a spectacular sight.

2

"Hey, Ma," I called out as I pulled our front door open and headed inside.

Thank God today was over; it'd been one of the longest days at work in a long time. We'd had lots of sick pets come in for emergency care, not to mention a couple of asshole customers. Scott Cole flashed through my mind as I thought of the assholes. Yeah, I'd totally memorised his name when he filled in his cat's paperwork. He was freaking hot; how could I not remember his name? But he wouldn't pass my checklist. What checklist, you might ask. The one I'd written after the last guy I dated cheated and lied his way through our three year relationship. That checklist. The one that forbade me to even look at a guy who oozed sex the way Scott did. I also didn't do guys who had a temper like his, guys who didn't love animals as much as I did, and I preferred single men with no children. Kids weren't a complete no go for me, but I could do without the added baggage. Oh, and not to forget the fact that he was a biker. I liked my men a little rugged but that was taking it to the extreme in my opinion. Never having met a biker before, I couldn't be sure, but the image I had in my mind was that of a chauvinistic, domineering man who couldn't commit to one woman. So, Scott was off limits. I mean, what kind of pet owner wouldn't bring their pet to the vet as soon as it got sick? Not the kind of man I wanted to date.

"I'm in the kitchen," my mother called out. I smiled; it was a good sign when she was in the kitchen after a day at work in a kitchen.

I found her a minute later, arm deep in dough. "You're making bread!" I loved her bread, as did lots of other people. My mum was renowned for her bread making skills. People from all over Brisbane flocked to her café to satisfy their desire for it. Well, they used to anyway. These days her café wasn't doing so well; it was the reason I'd recently moved back home with her. She needed help financially to keep her business afloat, so I'd come home to help her out. I now divided my time between my part time job at the vets and working with mum in her café. Besides, after I'd kicked that cheating asshole to the curb, leaving my life in Gympie behind hadn't been a hard thing to do. A fresh start was just what I needed.

She paused and looked up at me, her nose coated in flour and a look of total happiness on her face. When she broke out in a huge smile, my spirit soared. I hadn't seen her smile like that since I'd come home, and that had been three months ago. Watching my mother going through the motions of life but not feeling it had been a hard thing to do.

"I'm making bread," she said, simply, but there was nothing simple about that statement. Those three words told me so much more than just the fact she was making bread. This kitchen, and that bread was her happy place; a place she hadn't been in for too long.

I placed my handbag and keys on the kitchen table before making my way to the kettle to make a coffee. Mum's kitchen was huge with a big island bench in the centre where she did all her cooking. One side of the bench had stools and I pulled one out and sat on it after I put the kettle on.

"So, you had a good day. What happened?" I placed my elbows on the counter and rested my chin in my palms as I waited to hear what had brightened her day.

"A couple of restaurants placed standing orders for cakes today, and I picked up a stack of wedding cake orders too."

The other thing my mother was known for? You guessed it, cakes. They were to die for and I'd always been surprised that she didn't sell more than she did. I'd spent the last couple of weeks marketing her cakes to local businesses and it looked like my work was paying off.

"That's great. You'll have to teach me how to make

some of these cakes so that I can help you with the orders."

"Pfft, you don't need teaching. I already did that while you were growing up. Your baking skills are as good as mine, love."

"So, we're going to be busy making cakes. I really should try to find a night job so that I can work with you every day rather than at the vet's."

"Well, you know how I feel about you working there. That man treats you so badly and expects you to put up with a lot from his customers." My mother didn't like my boss and had tried many times to get me to quit my job, but I'd been looking for another job and there just wasn't anything out there at the moment. I needed a part time job to help my mum pay the bills; working full time in her café just wasn't financially possible yet.

"I know, Mum. I'm looking, I promise." The kettle boiled and I hopped up to make coffee for us both.

"Good," she said, as she continued to knead the dough. "Now, tell me about your day."

I WAS REMINDED of my promise to look for a new job the next morning when the first customer of the day abused me for the vet being late to work. Biting my tongue, I calmly made up an excuse for why my boss wasn't at work yet. I was quickly running out of excuses because this was becoming a common occurrence. So far, his whole family was either sick or dead, his car was ready for the scrap heap due to the number of times it had broken down and he'd suffered from enough illnesses that his immune system should have packed it in weeks ago. Yeah, I was over this; it really was time to ditch this job.

Four hours later, Scott Cole strode through the front doors and caused an explosion of sensations in my tummy. This was the last thing I wanted to feel when I saw him but a girl can't always control these things. Shit, I needed to get laid; it had been awhile and even longer since a guy had actually managed to get me to scream without faking it. I bet Scott would have me screaming all night long with no faking required. Just looking at him turned me on; god he was built. I could happily sit for hours letting my eyes roam over those muscles. His hair was light brown and cut close to his head; another turn on for me because really, you didn't want hair to get in the way of a good time, right? I'd had friends who loved guys with long hair, but I always wondered if all that hair would just be in the way when he got down and dirty. Yeah, give me really short hair any day. Now, the thing that really did me in where Scott was concerned; his lips. They were full and pouty, and I shivered at the thought of what those lips could do to me. My gaze dropped to his chest and I took in his tight black t-shirt and his biker vest. I'd seen the name of his club on the back of it yesterday when he left; the Storm Motorcycle Club.

The vest was the only thing about Scott that did nothing for me.

"I've come to collect Monty," he stated, like I may have forgotten which pet was his. Not likely. I doubted anyone ever forgot Scott; there was an indescribable something about him that was not easily forgotten. He projected male dominance and total confidence, along with a don't-fuck-with-me attitude. Actually, Scott was unlike any man I'd ever met before. Sure, I'd dated some guys that had that alpha personality about them, but Scott was alpha to the extreme from what I'd seen. He filled the room when he was in it; his presence totally dominated it and commanded your attention.

I decided to play with him a little; partly to see how he would handle it and partly because I was bored out of my mind. "Monty who?"

Confusion fleetingly crossed his face before the self-assured mask he seemed to wear so well was back in place. "Funny."

I shrugged. "Some customers would find it funny but something tells me that you don't have much of a sense of humour." As soon as the words were out of my mouth, I regretted them. Shit, it was bad enough to insult a customer, but to insult this badass could be taking it too far.

His eyes widened. Bugger. I waited for him to erupt; I hadn't forgotten that temper of his. But then a smirk slowly appeared and the tension left me, to be replaced with butterflies. Yeah, he was one sexy man, especially when he looked at me like that. "You'd be right with that assumption. And it shocks the shit out of me that I find you amusing, but I do."

Well, colour me surprised. I cocked my head to the side and smiled at him. He was a bit of an enigma to me; so far I knew that he was the kind of man who disliked rudeness, but also the kind of man who didn't look out for his sick pet. He had a temper on him and didn't hesitate to threaten a stranger, but he also treated his kid with such gentleness and kindness. This was one complex man. He smiled back, and oh my freaking god, when that dimple popped, I swear my panties almost caught on fire.

That dimple managed to scramble my thoughts, so I was sure I looked like a complete idiot when I said, "Uh, yeah, I'll just go get Monty for you." I scurried out to the back without a second glance at Scott; I didn't need to confirm how stupid I must have just looked.

A couple of minutes later, I placed the cat cage we'd put Monty in, onto the front counter. "Here he is; all better."

Scott took one look at Monty and then his eyes flew to mine. "What the fuck happened to his face?"

"Sorry, I should have mentioned that before I brought him out. We had to remove some of his skin because it had died. We've flushed the wound and now we need any further infection to drain out, so we've left the wound open. You'll need to keep it clean as the pus and blood drain from it. Just use a cloth to wipe it away.

Also, keep this collar on him so that he can't scratch or lick the wound, which he will try to do. He's been given antibiotics so he's well on his way to a complete recovery now."

Scott's full focus was on what I was saying. Even though he'd taken his sweet time to bring Monty in, I felt certain that he would do everything to make sure his cat recovered quickly. "Jesus, the poor fuckin' cat. Okay, I'll be calling you if I hit trouble with this; he's not getting this sick again."

I nodded. "Good, and yes, please don't hesitate to call us if you feel he's not recovering."

Scott pulled out his wallet. "Right, how much do I owe you?"

I pulled up his invoice on the computer. "For the operation, anesthetic and antibiotics, it comes to a total of five hundred and seventy dollars please."

"Fuck me! You sure that's right?"

"Yes," I replied, wondering if I was going to have an argument on my hands. I sighed. This was the least favourite part of my job; arguing with pet owners who didn't want to spend the money to get their pet better.

He shook his head and ran his hand over his hair, visibly annoyed, but he handed over his credit card. "Christ, I hope he won't need a follow up appointment."

I put the payment through and gave him his card back. "You'll need to bring him back in ten days, but there won't be a fee. We just need to take out the couple of stitches he does have and check to make sure he's healing. It'll only be a very quick visit," I assured him.

"Okay, so we're done here?" he asked as he lifted the cat cage.

"Yes," I replied.

"Thanks for your help. I'll return your cage as soon as I can."

I waved my hand at him. "No rush, you can bring it back when you bring Monty back in."

He gave me one last dimple inducing smile before turning and walking towards the door. As he got to it, he stopped and swung his head back to face me. "You have any more trouble with that asshole from yesterday?"

"No, I haven't heard from him."

"Good. Remember what I said; call me if you do. Pricks like him need a boot up their ass."

I smiled. He certainly had a way with words. "Thanks, will keep that in mind."

And then he was gone. And I turned my attention to my next patient, but thoughts of him throughout the day sent a thrill through me. Scott Cole was the kind of man that women like me threw their checklists out the window for.

3

SCOTT

I banged on Michelle's door and waited. It was the third time, and when she didn't answer, I yelled out, "Michelle, open the fucking door or I'm kicking it in." I didn't have time for this shit. It was nearly two o'clock and I had to get to Indigo within the next half hour to help J interview possible managers.

The door was flung open and I sucked in a breath as I took in Michelle's appearance. She was obviously high on something and looked like she hadn't showered in days.

"You've got to be fucking kidding me," I muttered, "I'm out there spending a shitload on your cat and you're here shooting shit into your arm."

"I didn't ask you to look after my cat," she snarled.

"Yeah, well someone had to do it or he would have fucking died."

"I don't give a shit about that fucking cat; he could have died for all I cared."

She's a chick, don't fucking hit her. I lowered my face down to hers. "You're a fucking pathetic excuse for a mother. Women like you should have their fucking legs sewn together."

Not waiting for her reply, I turned to leave.

"Anyone ever told you what an asshole you are?" she flung at me.

I turned back to look at her, "All the fucking time, bitch. And I'll continue being one until you get your shit together and give Lisa the care she fucking deserves."

I strode back to my car, still holding Monty in his cage. Fuck. I was going to have to take him to work with me until I sorted out someone to look after him. There was no way I was leaving him with Michelle now.

"A CAT? You brought a fucking cat with you?" J gave me shit when I hit Indigo twenty minutes later.

I placed the cat cage on the floor next to the desk in the office where we would be doing the interviews. "Michelle's off her face, and having just shed some serious coin on him, I didn't want to leave him with her. So yeah, brother, I'm bringing a fucking cat to work."

He chuckled, and rubbed his chin. "That kid's got you wrapped around her little finger."

"Shit! Is Madison working this afternoon?"

"No. Why?"

I reached in my pocket for my phone. "I want her to go over to Lisa's and let her know that I have Monty and that he's okay. She'll worry otherwise."

"I don't think she had anything planned so she should be able to do it."

I was just dialing her when Velvet poked her head around the door. "Scott, you got a minute?"

J jerked his head in Velvet's direction. "You go sort that out and I'll call Madison."

"Thanks," I said as I hung up and slipped my phone back in my pocket. "What's up?" I asked Velvet as I followed her towards the back storeroom.

"I think someone's tried to break in. The lock on the back door has been tampered with," she said.

"Fuck," I muttered as I inspected the lock. She was right; it had been messed with.

"Yeah, not good. And there were some guys hanging around last night that I've never seen before. Nasty looking fuckers."

I looked up at her. Velvet wasn't one to exaggerate. And she'd seen some shit in her life, so if she thought they were worth bringing to my attention, they were worth me worrying about. "Okay, I'll get Griff to take a look at the surveillance and I'll get some extra guys in to keep an eye on the joint. You let me know if you see them again."

"Thanks, Scott. And thanks for getting rid of Darrell."

"Was my fucking pleasure. Anyone else you want me to get rid of? With the mood I'm in, I'd be happy to go a couple of rounds with anyone who needs sorting out."

She laughed. "Mmmm, I think I'll steer clear of you for the rest of the day."

I watched as she walked away. Velvet was one sexy chick and our customers couldn't get enough of her. She had curves in all the right places, a seriously good set of tits and a spectacular ass that her long brunette hair almost hit. I didn't do staff though, so Velvet was firmly in the no go zone.

J entered the storeroom. "Madison can sort out the kid for you," he said as he came towards me.

I closed the back door and locked it. "Good. Thanks for organising that. Someone's fucked with the lock, and Velvet's seen some guys hanging around that I need to get Griff to look into."

"Christ, if it's not one thing, it's another," he said what I was thinking.

"Feels that way doesn't it."

He nodded. "Our first interview is here. You ready?"

I clapped him on the back, and smiled, "Yeah, brother. Let's see if we can pick a fucking winner this time."

∾

"So, I heard the interviews were a bust," Griff said, as he came behind the bar where I was pouring drinks. "And why the fuck are you making drinks? Don't we have staff for that?"

I finished pouring the beer and handed it to the customer. "Cheers," I said to him, and then gave my attention to Griff, "Not enough staff. Two of them called in sick tonight and I couldn't get hold of any of the others."

"Well, I'll leave you to it while I go and find out if we know these guys that Velvet mentioned. And, J said to tell you that Madison has that cat under control," he said, and then added, "He's pissed that it's staying at their house which amuses me no fucking end."

"Someone has to look after it because Michelle sure as shit won't and I can't have it here all night while I'm working."

He nodded, a frown coming over his face, "Yeah, that bitch is a sorry excuse for a human," he said as he started to walk away. "I'll let you know what I find."

I lifted my chin at him. "Thanks," I replied before going back to my customers.

It was just after eleven pm; I'd been here for nearly nine hours now and I'd had enough. How people managed to do this shit for a living was beyond me. People were so fucking rude; I'd had to walk away a few times tonight to avoid punching some of them. I needed to find new staff real fucking quick.

"Scott, it's slowed down a bit. Why don't you leave

me to the bar for a bit. Go and take a break," Amy suggested. She was my only bar staff for the night and she was right. She could handle it on her own now so I left her to it.

I wandered over to the table that Nash was sitting at. He'd been here for about an hour and was kicking back, enjoying the show. Diverting his attention from the girls for a minute, he eyed me and asked, "Why the fuck didn't you get one of the guys to work the bar tonight?"

"I'm running out of staff fast and I didn't want to chance one of the boys pissing any of the girls off. We can't afford to lose anymore staff."

"At least it's a quiet night."

"Yeah, thank fuck because I couldn't handle many more rude pricks tonight."

I looked up as Amy made her way over to the table with a beer in hand. "That for me?" I asked.

She nodded, "Thought you could use it."

"Thanks," I said as I took it from her, throwing some back without hesitation.

She laughed. "No problem, I'll get you another one after I serve these customers," she promised before heading back to the bar where there were two guys waiting for service.

"Spent some time today with Marcus trying to sort out this shit between Blade and Black Deeds. It was one big dick around. I don't think Blade's going to halt his operation, and I think it's going to end up in one big blood bath with us in the fuckin' middle," Nash said after she left us.

"Fuck," I muttered, "I don't trust him. Christ knows where this will all end up."

"He's unpredictable, that's for sure. Not much more we can do though."

I drank some more beer and nodded in agreement. "Yeah, and we've got enough other shit to take care of at the moment."

We sat in silence for awhile, watching the girls do their thing. Well, I was looking in their direction but I wasn't really watching. Nash was; he loved this shit, but it didn't do much for me anymore. A man could get tits and ass anywhere he wanted; I craved something different these days. Problem was, I didn't know what it was that I wanted; I just knew it wasn't this.

Jodie, one of the strippers appeared in front of us. "You boys want a private show?" she purred, thrusting her bare tits forward, hands on her hips. I knew that Nash had gone a few rounds with her and judging by the disinterested look on his face, his dick wasn't interested in any more from her.

"Not tonight, we've got club stuff to discuss," I replied firmly so that she got the message to leave us alone. Jodie was well known for harassing club members when they were here, and I didn't have it in me tonight to deal with her.

Looking at Nash, she said, "Well, if you change your mind, you know where to find me."

It was time to hammer the message home. "No-one's changing their mind so I suggest you get back to your pole. We clear?"

Now she turned her glare to me, and she didn't look pleased. "You can be a real asshole sometimes, Scott."

I stood up, and moved into her space. "Been told that already today, Jodie, and it's completely fucking true. I employ you to shake your ass at our customers, not to throw your self at club members who aren't interested. Now, get back to work before I find someone to replace you," I thundered, letting loose the anger I'd been holding in for hours.

She was visibly shaken at my outburst but that was too fucking bad; I'd had it with people today. Taking a step back, she hissed, "You're going to lose your best girls if you talk to them like that. The sooner you find a new manager the better." She blasted me with a foul glare and then turned and stomped back to the stage.

Sitting back down, I placed my hands behind my neck, and stretched my aching back. "Fuck," I muttered.

Nash chuckled. "She's right, asshole. You need to rein it in if you're going to manage this joint till you find someone else to do it. Dealing with people is not your strong point."

I scowled at him. "I know, and I'm fucking trying here, okay," I retorted, and then grumbled, "Shit."

4

I looked up from what I was doing when the door bell sounded. It was Madison, one of my favourite customers. A nice way to start the day.

"Hey, Harlow," she greeted me with a huge smile. She'd been coming here for a couple of months now and I always looked forward to her daily visits to collect coffee. Sometimes she came in with her brother, Blade, but he wasn't with her today. I was thankful for this; he scared the crap out of me. They seemed so different to each other. Madison came across as a warm, fun person, whereas her brother seemed dark and serious.

I smiled at her. "How's your day going?" I was already making her coffee because I knew from memory how she took it; skinny cappuccino, no sugar.

She dumped her huge handbag on the counter and sighed. "I haven't been in the last two days because J's back, finally. It's so good to have him home but getting into a routine together is kinda hard. I'm working some long hours at the dress shop at the moment and J's busy getting back into his work which is keeping him out at all hours. So, even though he's home, I feel like I've hardly spent any time with him." She paused and gave me a rueful look. "Sorry to whine."

From what I could work out, her boyfriend had been away for a couple of months. Although she'd been upset about it, she'd still seemed upbeat and happy. I figured Madison was one of those people who made the best out of whatever life handed her; she seemed like a strong person and I really liked that about her. She didn't complain about stuff too often so I figured she must really need to vent. "No, go ahead. Get it out."

I placed her coffee in front of her and she rummaged in her bag for some money. She was always rifling through her huge ass bag and I often wondered why she didn't replace it with a smaller one. After she found what she was looking for, she handed the four dollars over to me and I rang the sale up.

Waving her hand at me, she said, "I've finished; that was all I had to whine about." She drank some of her coffee and a glazed look came over her face. "Seriously girl, you make the best damn coffee in Brisbane, I swear."

"Thanks, love. I just wish more customers thought that too." I bent over and leant on the counter. "Mum's really struggling to make ends meet and even though we've picked up some new orders for cakes, I worry how she's going to pay her bills."

Madison contemplated that for a moment. "Maybe I can get my brother to consider using you to make the cakes for his restaurants."

"I didn't know that Blade owned restaurants."

"No, not Blade. My other brother. He runs four restaurants. I'm sure I can twist his arm to take on your cakes. If not, I'll get to him through J," she said, winking at me.

"Is J close to your brother?" Her family sounded pretty close although I didn't really know anything about them.

"God yes, they're best mates. Sometimes it irritates the fuck out of me."

A shot of jealousy ran through me. I envied people with extended family; my father had died when I was young and it was only my mother and I left after that. It would have even just been good to have a brother or sister. "Must be nice though. I mean, you hear stories about in-laws who hate each other and rip families apart, so for your brother and your boyfriend to get on that well would make it easier."

She nodded. "Yeah, you're right there. Hey, what you are you doing on Sunday?"

"I've got the day off. Why?"

"I'm having a barbeque at my house and I want you to come."

This surprised me; we weren't exactly friends. "Ah, sure."

She laughed. "I know that we don't know each other very well but I'd like to get to know you better. You up for it?"

When she put it like that, I realised that I'd like to get to know her more too. I didn't have a lot of friends in Brisbane yet. "I'm in. What do you want me to bring?"

"Just yourself and anything you want to drink."

"How about I bring some cake too?" I'd make one of Mum's red velvet cakes. They were always a hit at parties.

"Sure, honey. That sounds great." She started searching through her bag again, retrieving her phone. "I better go otherwise I'll be late for work. Thanks for the coffee. I'll probably see you tomorrow." Swiping her keys off the counter, she turned to leave but then looked back at me. "Thanks for listening to me whinge. I don't have many friends in Brisbane so it's nice to have you. I'd better get your phone number and then I can text you my address."

Smiling, because she'd said what I'd been thinking too, I rattled off my number for her. She keyed it in to her phone and then thanked me one last time before leaving to go to work. I was really looking forward to Sunday now; meeting Madison's family and friends would be fun if they were even half as nice as her. Her boyfriend, J, intrigued me; I wasn't sure what he did for a living or why he was away for so long, but the way that Madison talked about him made me think he was a nice guy.

5

SCOTT

Juggling a tray of steaks, a tray of sausages and a huge bottle of tomato sauce, I strode through J's front door and down the hall towards the back of his house. Out of the corner of my eye, I vaguely took in the paint tins on the floor near the back door and the pile of paint chips on the kitchen table. Madison must have gotten her way; she wanted to repaint the house but I knew that J hadn't been keen. She had him wrapped around her little fucking finger.

I placed the food on the kitchen bench and surveyed the back yard where they had everything set up. J had a large undercover area outside; it was usually where we liked to drink and shoot the shit but now that Madison was around, I could see more of these barbeques happening.

"Scott, you made it," Madison said as she

approached the back door from outside. "Did you bring the meat?"

"Yeah, you want it outside now?"

"Not yet. Why are you late?" She slid the door open and came inside.

"I had to deal with Lisa's cat again. That fucking cat has a death wish and it doesn't help that Michelle couldn't give a shit."

Madison started pulling food out of the fridge and then said, "God, I dislike that woman so much. What happened to Monty now?"

I leant against the counter. "He got out of the house when he should have been inside. Then he climbed a fucking tree and I had to get him down."

She started laughing. "You climbed a tree?" she asked.

"Yes, I climbed a tree. The fucking cat jumped down so it was a waste of time. Anyway, Lisa caught him and got him back inside. So, crisis averted, but I had strong words with Michelle. That bitch really needs to get her shit together."

Madison went quiet and I knew what she was thinking. I reached out and lifted her chin so she was looking at me rather than the floor. "You're nothing like her. You're working on your shit, handling it; she doesn't give a fuck. And she should because she's got a kid. Okay?"

Nodding, she said quietly, "Yes, but I still feel like

she just needs someone to help her; someone who cares enough to show her what she's doing."

I shoved my hand through my hair. "Christ, we've done that. Nash, Griff and me... we all tried to get her to own up to her shit before we fired her. The thing is, if someone doesn't want help, there's not much anyone can do. She needs to hit bottom before she'll see it. Either that or she'll be dead without ever seeing it and I hope to God that doesn't happen for Lisa's sake."

"But at what point do you give up on someone? Would you have given up on me?"

"No, but you wanted help and took it. And you're my sister."

"Doesn't Michelle have any family who are looking out for her?"

"I don't know, but if she does, they're not around. I've only ever seen her junkie friends hanging around her house."

"Maybe I should go over and see her; try and get her some help."

My sister had always been a bleeding heart. "Sure, but don't be surprised when she spits in your face or tries to screw you over."

She finished getting the food out of the fridge and I was just about to help her take it outside when Nash came through the back door. "Hey, motherfucker, where you been?"

"Getting meat for your sorry ass," I replied, taking the beer he passed me.

"Stoney's brought some girls along and they seem ready to party, so you need to get outside because you're a cranky fuck when you go this long without a hit of pussy."

I took a long swig of my beer and scowled at him. "I'm not interested in any chick that Stoney's brought with him. Fuck knows what's been up in that."

"That's why you wrap it brother, and fuck, so long as there's tits and ass who cares who brought them?"

"Guys, do I really need to listen to this?" Madison glared at me with that look of hers that said to shut it.

Nash smirked at her. "Sweet thing, you live with J. Seriously, you can't tell me you don't hear him talking like this. That fucker's mouth is dirty."

Now she glared at Nash. "It might be dirty, Nash, but I don't have to listen to him discussing screwing other women like they're a piece of meat."

"When I fuck a woman, the last thing she feels like is a piece of meat."

The back door slid open and J stepped into the room as Nash spoke. He looked pissed. "Nash, why the fuck are you telling Madison about your sex life? She doesn't need to hear that shit."

The room was full of tension now, with J and Nash having a stand-off. Madison threw her arms up and declared, "Okay, enough." She pointed at Nash, "You, outside, back to your skanks." Then she pointed at me, "You, go with him and take these." She piled plates with cheese, dips and other shit on them in my arms. Lastly, she pointed at J, her face softening as she gave him her attention. "You can help me in here."

Nash grumbled something I couldn't catch, and then did as he was told. I followed him, leaving J and Madison alone. From what J had told me the other day, they needed some time together to sort their shit out so I wasn't keen to interrupt that.

The chicks that Stoney had brought with him were exactly what I expected. There were three of them, each with bleached blonde hair, overdone makeup and the shortest and tightest dresses you could imagine. One was sitting on Stoney's lap; the other two looked expectantly at Nash and I as we approached.

Stoney lifted his chin at me. "Hey, VP. I brought some friends." He rattled off their names but I wasn't listening. Nash was all over them though and thank fuck for that because that meant they were leaving me alone.

I spread the dips out on the table, sat down and kicked back with my beer. Besides Stoney and Nash, there were some other couples here who I didn't know. I figured they were friends of Madison. They were sticking to themselves and didn't seem interested in talking to us. Again, fine by me; I was enjoying being left alone. It had been a long week dealing with Indigo and other Storm business. Blade was still pissing Bullet off, and in return, Bullet was breathing down our necks to pull him into line. Dad was fucking around with the whole thing; leading Storm into dangerous territory because when Bullet was pissed off, he had a nasty way of dealing with it. On top of that, we still hadn't found a manager for Indigo.

As I contemplated all the Storm shit going on, the chicks that Nash had been occupying got up and went inside. I watched them go and then looked over at him. "What'd you say to them?"

"Nothing, they'll be back in a minute," he answered and then suddenly sat up straight in his chair, eyes trained on the kitchen. "Holy fuck, look at that fine piece of ass."

I glanced in the direction he was looking, not really interested because, let's be honest, Nash and I had totally different tastes in women.

"Well, I'll be fuckin' damned," I whistled under my breath. Standing in the kitchen, talking to Madison, was none other than Harlow, the hot blonde from the vet.

Nash twisted his head to face me. "You know her?"

I nodded slowly. "Yeah, she works with the vet that I just donated a shitload of money to."

"Fuck, I want to tap that," he said as he stood.

I quickly stood also, and grabbed his arm to stop him. "She's not your type, Nash."

"I don't have a type, brother. She's got a hot ass, a great rack and I bet there's a sweet pussy to go with all that; I'd say that's my type."

He shrugged my hand off his arm and walked towards Harlow. I sat back down and observed. Harlow was wearing a short denim skirt and a tight black tank top with a shitload of necklaces again. I could do without those necklaces; they blocked the view. While Nash chatted to her I took in the way she twirled her hair between her fingers as she listened. He would have her under his spell within minutes; he was a smooth motherfucker. She laughed. *Yeah, brother, home run.*

As they continued to talk, Madison and J came outside, carrying the meat I'd brought with me. J looked at me and jerked his head towards the barbeque to indicate he wanted my help. I met him there and muttered, "Madison doesn't intend on having these things too often, does she?"

"Fuck, I hope not. The last thing I want to be doing on a weekend is entertaining her stuck up work friends but you know what your sister is like; when she wants something to happen, it fucking happens."

"Time to put your foot down, brother, and say no."

"And risk getting cut off? Not fucking likely. I've been cranking the shank for long enough."

"You're a pussy."

"You wait till you rely on one woman and then let's see how quick you are to ever piss her off."

"And that's a good reason to never rely on one woman, J. Relationships aren't for me."

He chuckled. "One day, brother. One day you're gonna fall and I can't fucking wait to see it."

I ignored him and moved on to discuss Indigo business. J had lined up more manager interviews for next week; we were desperate to find someone for the job so we could spend less time fucking about with the day to day running of the joint. When Storm bought Indigo, it was purely as an investment opportunity; there was a manager in place and we wanted nothing to do with running it. We just wanted to collect the cash at the end of each month. Now it had turned into one gigantic headache.

We finished cooking the meat and I carried it over to the table where Madison had set the food up. Stoney was deep in conversation with the three chicks he'd brought with him, although one of them was distracted by Nash and Harlow who were still standing inside talking.

"Nash, time to get your ass out here and eat," J called out to him. Harlow turned her head and surprise crossed her face when she saw me. She quickly gave her attention back to Nash but after saying something to him, they both looked at me. I decided to join their conversation.

Walking towards them, I said, "How do you know Madison, Harlow?" I slid the door open and took a moment to appreciate the curves that Harlow was made of.

"My eyes are up here," she said. I ignored the tone she took with me.

Meeting her eyes, I said, "You didn't answer my question."

"That's because I like to look someone in the eye when I'm speaking to them. Madison is a customer at my Mum's café. She loves the coffee. So does her brother."

What the fuck? "I'm her brother, sweetheart." I hadn't realised that Madison and Blade were spending that amount of time together. "Blade's our half brother."

She looked like she was connecting dots in her mind. "So you're the brother who owns restaurants and is best mates with J. Yes?"

"Shit, let me guess, you know our entire family history too." Why did women feel it necessary to share so much with each other?

Nash chuckled. "Madison likes to talk, brother."

"No, I don't know your family history. What's wrong with knowing a couple of things about a friend's family?" She was peeved.

"I just don't understand why women talk so much about private shit."

"It's because we like to get to know each other. I don't understand why men don't talk at all." She folded her arms across her chest and I dropped my gaze to take in the cleavage on display.

"We do; we just don't waste breath on bullshit."

Her face was ablaze with annoyance. It was hot, and it fucking turned me on.

"Are you always this much of an asshole?"

"Oh, baby, you ain't seen nothing yet," Nash snickered.

"No actually, I think I've seen enough." Her voice was coated in ice. She gave me one last dirty look before pushing past me to go outside to Madison. I zeroed in on her ass as she walked away, imagining what it would look like without that skirt covering it.

"Fuck, I've never seen a woman dismiss you like that before. She either hates you or totally wants to fuck you. I'm going with the hates you option because I'm betting she actually wants to fuck me, not you," Nash surmised.

His words faded into the background as I continued to track Harlow's movements. Nash was right; women didn't fucking walk away from me. But more to the point; I didn't chase them, so I diverted my gaze away from her and looked at Nash. He was watching me with a smirk on his face.

"What?" I demanded.

"Like I said, I've never seen a chick walk away from you, but I've also never seen you make the effort to check one out. You got a hard on for that one?"

Scowling, I said, "Highly fucking unlikely. She's got a hot ass but there's plenty of hot asses out there for the taking."

He laughed. "Whatever you say, brother. Whatever you say."

I ignored him and looked at J who was motioning for us to come and eat. "Let's go and eat and get this over with. The sooner the better as far as I'm concerned."

"MADISON TOLD me you're still dealing with that cat and Michelle," J said midway through lunch.

"Yeah, the bitch is high all the time and has no idea what's going on with her daughter or her cat."

Madison leant over to Harlow who was sitting next to her. "That's the cat he brought into your work." We'd worked out the connection between us all, but Harlow still looked confused. She was sitting across from me and was eyeing me strangely. It looked like she had something to say but wasn't sure how to say it.

"Spit it out," I said gruffly.

"Spit what out."

"Whatever the fuck is running through your mind right now. Looks to me like you've got something to say." Jesus, she'd been shooting me filthy looks all lunch and my patience was wearing thin. I lived my life one way; if you've got something to say, then fucking say it.

She huffed, displeasure clear as day on her face. "I'm just confused as to why you leave your child with a woman who is high. And your cat too."

Anger flashed through me at her judgmental attitude. I leaned forward and stared her hard in the face. "You should get your facts straight before you go shooting your mouth off. For one, Lisa isn't my kid. Two, that cat isn't mine either. And three, the last place I would leave Lisa, if I could help it, would be with her own fucking mother."

Surprise flared across her face. "Oh."

"Yeah, oh is fucking right."

"Scott.." Madison tried to shut me up.

I shoved my chair back and stood up. "Yeah, I'm out. Thanks for lunch but I'm going to go."

"I'm sorry, Scott. Please don't leave because of what I said," Harlow apologised but I didn't really want to hear it; people had one shot with me and she'd said more than enough for me to work out the kind of person she was.

"I'm not leaving because of you but I'll be honest; I've got no interest in anything else you have to say."

Her eyes widened, and Madison sucked in a breath. She looked pissed off with me. "Fine. Go." Yeah, I was in my sister's bad books again but it was a place I was familiar with.

Without even bothering to say goodbye to J, Nash or Stoney, I left through the side gate. I stalked to my bike, gripped by anger, but I wasn't sure who the anger was directed at. And my suspicion that it was actually directed at myself only served to annoy me even more.

6

HARLOW

I sat in stunned silence. Scott had just stormed out of Madison's get together, because of me. I was mad at myself for causing this to happen, and really freaking shitty that I'd judged him incorrectly and actually voiced my thoughts out loud to him. It was so out of character for me to do that. I was the kind of woman who thought stuff about people but never had the guts to say it to their face. Keeping the peace was high on my agenda in life. For me to say what I'd said to Scott was so far out of left field for me that I was sitting here stewing on it and trying to work out why I'd opened my mouth.

Everyone else had just carried on as if nothing had happened after he left. This also surprised me. Not one of them got up and followed him to try and get him to stay. The more I thought about it, the more I felt the urge to go and catch him before he left, and apologise again.

I quickly stood, grabbing Madison's attention as I did this. "What's wrong, honey?" she asked.

"I'm going to go and apologise to Scott again. I feel awful about what I said."

She waved her hand dismissively. "Pfft, don't worry about him. Scott's a moody bastard; it's best just to let him go when he's like this."

Well that would explain why no-one was going out of their way to stop him from leaving. However, I still wanted to try apologising again. "No, I'm just going to see if he's still out the front. I won't be long."

I followed the path he'd taken when he left, and hurried out the front. When I saw him sitting on his bike, I felt both relief and apprehension about approaching him. His face was a mask of anger and the moodiness that Madison spoke of was rolling off him. I stalled for a moment, but then threw caution to the wind and walked to where he was.

He must have heard me because he whipped his head around and turned his angry eyes on me. I held up my hands in a defensive gesture. "Just hear me out, okay?"

A minute passed as he contemplated this and then he nodded.

"I truly am sorry for what I said, Scott. Yes, I presumed you were Lisa's father and Monty's owner. Yes, I thought you were a shitty pet owner for not bringing him in sooner. And yes, I presumed that Lisa's mother was your partner and that you were happy to leave Lisa with someone who was high all the time. Which then led me to the conclusion that you were a crappy father and human being -"

He cut me off. "Is that supposed to be a fucking apology? Because if it is, it's the worst one I've ever heard."

"No, this is the apology bit. I'm sorry that I judged you. You have no reason to believe me or even care, but I'm not usually this judgmental. In fact, if you were to ask any of my friends or family they would say I was the least judgmental person they know. They would also tell you that I never, ever speak my thoughts like I did to you. I have no idea what came over me today."

He held up his hand to stop me. He didn't seem as angry anymore. "As far as I'm concerned, you should always speak your mind. I'm not pissed that you did that. But as for judging me, yeah, that shit me. However, I've been sitting here thinking about it, and as much as I fucking hate to admit it, I can see how you could have come to the conclusion you came to."

"So, apology accepted?" I asked, pushing him. He didn't seem like the kind of man to easily accept an apology.

He hesitated for a moment. "Yeah."

He gave me a one word answer, and yet it felt like he'd given me something rare. I didn't know Scott well enough to know for sure, but I sensed from his body language that he didn't really want to give what he'd given.

I waited for him to get off his bike but instead, he moved to put his helmet on. "Are you still leaving?" I asked, and realised that I wanted him to stay.

He stopped putting his helmet on and gave me a pointed look. "I don't do get togethers. Only came to this one because Madison would get pissy if I didn't, and Madison in a pissy mood isn't worth the headache. You gave me a good excuse to leave."

I laughed. "Glad I could help you out then."

"Yeah, thanks for that." There was a hint of humour in his voice and he sat watching me for a minute. Finally, he put the helmet on, turned on his bike and took off without a backwards glance.

I stood on the footpath for a long time staring after him. There was definitely something about Scott Cole; something that made long forgotten desires come to the surface. As I stood staring into the distance, I realised that I'd liked it when he just sat and watched me. His eyes hadn't moved from mine and somehow we'd connected. I'd felt it but I wondered if he had. I also wondered if it was even a good idea to be thinking these things because, let's face it, Scott was bound to be heartbreak on legs.

THE NEXT DAY, I sailed through my shift at the vets as

thoughts of Scott flitted in and out of my mind. I'd
memorised his muscles, the ink on his arms, his lips and
his eyes. These images were floating around my head all
day and I've gotta say, they made me a happy girl. Even
my boss's snarky attitude towards me all day couldn't
change my mood. Nor did thoughts of the bills my Mum
was facing in her café.

A couple of hours later though, I completely
changed my mind about Scott Cole. At the end of my
shift, my boss called me into his office.

"Harlow, I'm going to have to let you go. I've had a
complaint from Rod about the way he was treated the
other day. The way you dealt with that situation was
completely unacceptable," he said, as he shuffled papers
on his desk and did his best to avoid eye contact
with me.

My heart started beating faster, and heat flooded my
body. How dare he fire me over that idiot. "You're
kidding, right? You fire me without even getting my
version of what happened? Rod is one of the rudest
customers I've ever dealt with in my life, and you'll
regret choosing him over me!"

"I don't think so. He's one of my best customers;
that dog of his is always in here getting something done.
I can't afford to upset customers like him."

I picked up my handbag that I had placed on his
desk, and stood up. "You know what? I don't want to
work for an idiot like you anyway. I think this will be

for the best after all," I snapped, and then stormed out of his office.

As I drove home, I assessed the events of the last week and decided that Scott had screwed with my life. My mother and I counted on that income from my job at the vet to help cover her mortgage and her bills from the café. Unless I found a new job really soon, I worried that she wouldn't be able to cover all her bills, and wondered where that would leave us. If I ever saw Scott Cole again, I'd be sure to give him a piece of my freaking mind.

7

"**F**ucking hell!" I yelled as I rifled through the beer invoice that I was holding. Moving my eyes from the invoice to J, I continued, "How fucking hard is it for them to get an order right?"

J grabbed the invoice from me and assessed it. "Before you take that temper out on the supplier, you'd better check with our staff to make sure it wasn't them who fucked it up."

"Yeah, I'll do that, but brother, we need a new manager because neither of us is cut out for this shit."

"I hear you. I've got some more interviews to line up."

"Good."

J looked at his watch. "I've got to head home. Call me if something urgent comes up, otherwise I'm busy for the night. And when I say I'm busy, I mean with a woman who you don't want to fuck with."

I held up my hand. "I don't need to hear anymore. We won't be bothering you."

Nash wandered into the storeroom at that moment and the air thickened with tension as he and J watched each other. I'd thought that once Madison made it clear she was settling down with J, these two would start getting along but it didn't seem to be the case. If anything, they were getting along worse than ever.

"Marcus asked me to pass along that he thinks he's talked some sense into Blade. Thinks that Blade will pull back on his coke distribution," Nash shared.

"What makes him so sure?" I seriously doubted this was true. Blade had now had a taste of the money coke bought in; he wouldn't give that up so easily.

Nash shrugged. "Got no idea, brother. Just passing on the message."

As Nash and I talked, J walked towards the storeroom door. "I'll catch you later," he said to me, ignoring Nash.

We watched him leave and then I asked, "Why's he so dirty with you still?"

"Don't know and don't fucking care. J's an asshole who I have no time for."

"You still got a thing for Madison?"

"Fuck no, brother. She could do better than him though, and I haven't been backward in telling her that."

"I'd stay out of it now, if I was you. Now that J's home, you don't want to be fucking around where Madison's concerned," I warned him. There'd be hell to pay if J ever found out what Nash had been saying to Madison. And that was hell that our club didn't need.

"I've said my piece and I'm out of it. Got better things to do with my time anyway," he said with that Nash grin that meant only one thing; sex.

I chuckled; the mood now lighter. "I'm sure you fucking have, brother."

"We need to hook you up, VP. You're more moody than normal and some pussy will help that."

He was right. "Yeah, but let me do my own hooking up. I don't want the kind of bitches you'd find me."

"Pussy's pussy, brother."

"No it fucking isn't."

"When did you get so picky? I remember a time when you'd take anything and everything on offer. Wasn't so long ago."

"Christ, what the fuck is this, Nash? Quilting fucking circle? I don't want to sit around and dissect my sex life." I started walking out of the storeroom, towards the office.

Nash followed me and along the way we ran into Velvet. A scowl crossed her face when she saw Nash but she quickly hid it and turned her attention to me. "The place is hopping tonight and there's a shitload of dickheads in attendance. You might want to call in some more of your guys."

Just what we needed. "Will do. You up soon?" Being the star of our club, there was often some problems with drunk patrons when she performed. We were down some security tonight so I wanted to be out there ready for any issues when she was on.

"In about fifteen minutes," she answered me.

"How many boys you want me to call in?" Nash asked, his phone ready to go. Velvet was back to scowling at him which was strange. I thought these two were good friends.

"Get four of them in and tell them to hurry the fuck up," I said to Nash, my interest in what was happening between Nash and Velvet gone. So long as it didn't interfere with Storm or Indigo, I could care less about their issues with each other. "I'll be out there soon. I want to keep an eye on you tonight, just because we're down some men," I said to Velvet.

She looked happy with this news. "Thanks, boss," she said and then left Nash and I alone.

He finished up his call. "I'll go out and check what's happening."

"Sure. Be out soon."

He nodded and then left. I sat down at the desk in the office and spent a couple of minutes looking through invoices that needed payment or some kind of follow up. This part of the job was the shit part. We'd better have a new manager soon because it was headache material.

AN HOUR LATER, I was kicking back with a beer.

Velvet's performance had gone off without a hitch, our extra security had turned up and the place seemed to be under control. Nash was sitting across from me at the table; once again, enjoying the show. From where I was sitting, I could see the front door and I was surprised to see Harlow stumble through it. The friend she was with was also stumbling; they'd obviously been out drinking for the night. How the fuck they ended up in a strip club was anyone's guess. Harlow didn't strike me as your standard strip club patron. I stood up, watching her intently. She was making a beeline to the bar even though any fool could tell she had enough alcohol in her system to last her for a long time. Suddenly, our eyes met and a shitty look crossed her face. She changed her direction and started towards me.

She kept coming until she was almost in my face, and shoved a finger at my chest. "Scott freaking Cole!" she slurred, "You owe me big time. I lost my job because of you."

"What the fuck? Why?" I took a step back, to move away from her, but she stepped forward and maintained our closeness.

"You pissed that customer off and he put a complaint in about me. He's one of our best customers so the vet chose him over me. Thank you very freaking much!"

"He deserved everything I said to him," I defended myself although I wasn't sure why; it wasn't something I was ever compelled to do.

"Yeah, he's an asshole for sure, but you didn't have to get your dick out and wave it around like freaking King Shit, threatening him and all. I could have handled him by myself."

She jabbed her finger at my chest again and this time I stopped her and grabbed her hand. We were already close, but I tilted my head so our foreheads almost touched; our breath mingling. She smelt of bourbon mixed with some other smell that hit me right in the dick. *Christ.* "Babe, I'll get my dick out and wave it around like fucking King Shit anytime I fucking want. And I'll especially get it out whenever someone treats people the way that dickhead treated you. You didn't deserve that shit. So, don't come in here poking your finger at me and yelling at me for something that needed to be done."

Her eyebrows shot up and she sucked in a breath. Her lips parted and I could hear her short, choppy breaths as they quickened. I kept my eyes focused on hers, and we stayed locked like that for a moment, just watching each other, taking everything in. My senses were assaulted by her; all I could see, smell and hear was her. *And fuck if I didn't want a taste as well.*

I let her go but neither of us moved. Her eyes softened; the hard glare she'd been looking at me with a second ago, gone. A flush came over her cheeks and a hint of a smile touched her lips. When her tongue darted out and licked her lips, a sensation shot right through me and wrapped itself around my cock. It settled in the pit of my stomach a second later. *Fuck, what was that scent she was wearing?* It was screwing with my mind and my body. I resisted the urge to lean right into her and inhale it.

Harlow made the first move; she stepped back, right into Nash who was now standing behind her. He reached out to steady her, his hands gripping her hips. "Watch out, sweet thing, or you'll excite my ankle spanker even more than you already have."

Confusion flit across her face. "Your what?" she asked before turning around to look at him.

Nash's hands curved around Harlow's ass as she turned. I zeroed in on this, as well as her failure to remove them. I clenched my jaw and fists; ready to strike but not even sure why. Trying to fight the urge but not succeeding, I reached out and yanked Nash's hands off her ass. I then hooked my hand around her waist and pulled her back towards me, away from Nash. She gasped as she lost her balance but I held on tight to prevent her fall, and she ended up backed right against me. Nash just looked amused; probably wondering what the fuck I was doing. I knew I sure as hell was. Seeing Nash's hands on a woman was a normal occurrence for me so why was it any different when it was his hands on Harlow?

"Nash has a filthy mouth. You don't want to know half the shit he talks about," I murmured near her ear, her hair brushing across my face.

She made a noise that sounded like a moan before

mumbling, "Well, I'd like to know what an ankle spanker is."

I'd met a lot of women in my life. Hell, I'd fucked a lot of women in my life. They came and they went; I hardly remembered faces, never remembered names, and had no desire to know any of those women beyond the feel of their pussy wrapped around my dick. They would have all known what an ankle spanker was. Harlow stood there, blazing with naivety and I was damn sure her name and face were burned into my brain.

Letting her go, I waited until she turned slightly so she could see both Nash and I before telling her, "It's a huge cock, sweetheart. Nash here likes to consider himself well hung."

Her face flamed with redness. "Oh."

Nash grinned, and I scowled at him. He wasn't easily put off though, and indicated for Harlow and her friend to sit with us. "I'll get you some water, ladies," he said as he guided them into their seats.

Harlow's friend's eyes trailed up and down my body before she fixed a filthy stare on me. "This is the guy who lost you your job?"

Before Harlow could answer, Velvet appeared at the table. "Boss, we've got a slight issue at the front door. Might need your help."

Reluctantly diverting my attention from Harlow, I nodded at Velvet. "Be right back," I said to Harlow before heading to the front of the club.

My blood boiled the instant I hit the footpath outside. A couple of people were milling around a chick who was sitting on the ground crying. Her cheek was swollen and painted with blood. I flicked my glare to our bouncer who had a guy up against the wall. I stormed over to them and pulled the guy around so he was facing me.

I jerked my chin towards the chick on the ground. "You do that, asshole?"

His cold eyes challenged me, giving me all the information I needed. I pulled my arm back and landed a punch on his cheek. His face swung to the side from the impact and his body slightly crumpled. I took the opportunity to get another couple of punches in; on his face and then his ribs. I fed off the grunts of pain he emitted and the cracking sounds my fists caused when they connected with his body. If it wasn't for Nash pulling me off him, I would have kept going.

"Easy, brother," Nash muttered as he shoved me backwards.

I pointed at the asshole. "If I ever fucking see you here again, your legs won't get you home. Women aren't put on this earth to be your punching bag. Now, get the fuck out of my sight," I thundered.

Turning my attention to the chick on the ground, I said, "You want me to organise someone to take you to the hospital?"

She shook her head, and her friend declined my

offer, "Thanks, but we've got it under control. A friend's just gone to get his car."

"Good," I said, and then asked, "He your boyfriend?"

She nodded but didn't say a word. Her eyes fell to the ground and she looked ashamed.

I knelt down next to her. "This wasn't your fault. I have no idea what's gone on between you two but nothing you've said or done gives that asshole the right to take to you with his fists. You got that?"

She nodded again but her eyes betrayed her; she didn't believe what I'd said for one second.

"Let me guess, this shit goes on often and you keep going back for more. You're worth more than that scumbag piece of shit. If you start believing that one day and need help to get back on your feet, you come see me. Until then, I fucking hope you survive the next round because, let me tell you, it's just gonna keep coming till you decide to put a stop to it."

I stood back up and left her there. There was nothing else to say; no-one could do for this chick what she needed to do for herself. My breath would be wasted if I kept talking; kinda like with my mother.

"All sorted," I said to Velvet as I walked past her on my way back to Harlow.

Harlow and her friend were at the bar chatting with Amy. I let my gaze drop to Harlow's ass as she leant over the counter to tell Amy something. Tonight she was wearing a black dress that barely covered anything and clung to her curves in all the right fucking places. And fuck, she had some serious curves going on. I didn't do really skinny chicks; I didn't see the point if they've got nothing to grip on to. My eyes trailed down her legs; long legs that would feel good around me. And those heels she was wearing? Fuck, I'd like to take everything else off and just leave those in place; my back would love them digging into it while I pumped into her.

She looked up at me as I approached. "So, you're the boss here? I think you should give me a job. Amy tells me you need staff and I'm unemployed. As you know."

I didn't miss the emphasis on that last sentence, and was sure to throw Amy a dirty look. Harlow would be as suited to this job as a nun would be to a prostitute.

"You've had one too many drinks, sweetheart, and have no clue what you're saying at the moment. You don't want to work here."

She planted her hands on her hip, and gave me what I imagined was her best 'you've got to be kidding' look. "You don't know anything about me. How do you know where I want to work?"

"I know enough to know that you wouldn't cope with men leering at you and pawing you while you served them drinks."

"You might be surprised. I've met some assholes in my time and I've put them in their place."

"I'm sure you have, but the answer's still no. I don't need to be worrying about you all the time."

"No-one asked you to worry about me."

"Christ, do you ever take no for an answer?" I asked; irritation battling with a slight sense of respect.

"No. So give me the damn job already."

Amy drew her breath in and Nash stepped forward and touched Harlow on the arm. "Sweet thing, I think he's made himself clear."

"Yeah, I've made myself really fucking clear," I growled.

Harlow shook him off, and stepped closer to me, her green eyes hard. "I don't get you. I need a job, you need staff, it's a no brainer. All I'm asking for is an interview..."

"Are you fucking finished?" I roared, fury dripping from my words.

She stiffened, and moved her hand to her throat. Those greens of hers widened for a second before she narrowed them and replied, "Yes."

She made a move to step away from me but I reached out and grabbed her hard by the wrist to stop her. "I don't owe you a fucking explanation but you're going to get one anyway. I do need staff but I would prefer experienced staff. And staff who are suited to working in a strip club. When I say I don't have a job for you, it's because I don't believe you'd enjoy it and I don't think it would be a good fit for you." I let her go, and said to Amy, "Can you make sure these two get in a cab?"

Amy nodded. "Sure."

Giving Harlow one last look, I said, "You don't belong in a place like this. Go home, sleep those drinks off and find a nice job, far away from here."

I left them all standing there and stalked to the office. My mind was overwhelmed. Between my father, Indigo, Blade, Black Deeds and other Storm business, I was buckling under the pressure. Harlow prancing in here with her fucking curves, attitude and inclination to challenge me at all stops was something I was unable to deal with tonight.

And fuck it, I still wanted a taste of her.

W as that a jackhammer? The noise coming from outside my house was so freaking loud that I thought my skull might explode. I slowly opened my eyes and pain tore through my head as the light was allowed in. Scrunching them shut again, I prayed for the pain to end. It didn't; it only intensified.

Bloody hell, I was never, ever drinking again.

The noise from outside sounded again, along with a, "Harlow!"

I sat up in bed, the pain ricocheting from side to side at my sudden movement. That sounded like Scott. I threw the sheet off me and slowly got out of bed. My hand flew to my head to try and hold it; if I could keep it still it wouldn't hurt as much. That was my theory anyway. Hangovers weren't something I often dealt with; I'm sure that made it feel worse.

On second thoughts, maybe I should drink more often.

"Harlow! You in there?" Yep, definitely Scott.

I made my way to the front door because I was sure he would keep banging and yelling until I did. When I finally opened the door, the sun smacked me in the face and I winced as I tried to cover my eyes with my hand.

"Fuck," Scott muttered, and I parted two fingers so I could peer at him through the slit. His eyes were focused on my legs and then they lazily moved up to my face, lingering on my breasts as they went. A jolt of electricity shot through me. Scott Cole's eyes undressing me made me wet. His hands ripping my clothes off would surely make me scream.

"Do you always answer your door wearing nothing?" he demanded roughly, stepping into my house and moving me out of the way so that he could shut the door behind us.

I looked down at what I was wearing. Bloody hell, he was right. I was only wearing my thong and a tiny tank. Swallowing my mortification, I carried on as if this was a normal occurrence even though it was as far from my usual behavior as you could get.

"Do you always wake people up by banging on their door and yelling at them? Especially when you know that they would have a hangover and need complete silence to get through the day?"

He smirked, so I smacked him in the arm, and then sashayed my way down the hall; making sure to give him an eyeful of my bare ass. I figured I may as well work with the situation at hand even if it wasn't what I would have chosen. The noise he made as he sucked in a breath was almost enough to make up for my embarrassment.

When I reached the end of the hall, I pointed left towards the kitchen. "You go in there and I'll be with you in a minute." Turning right, I hurried to my bedroom so I could put some clothes on. My head was hammering, I felt queasy, and I was still annoyed at the way he spoke to me last night, but I couldn't deny the excitement bubbling through me that Scott was in my house.

A couple of minutes later, dressed more appropriately in shorts, a t-shirt and a bra, I found him with his head in the fridge. He heard me and stuck his head out, looking at me, body still bent over. "You got any cold water in here?"

I shook my head. "No, I don't drink cold water."

"Juice?"

"No."

He shut the fridge, grabbed a glass out of the dish rack, filled it with water from the tap and brought it to me. Then he walked back to the kitchen bench where he'd put his keys. I sat at the table, wondering what he was doing, but as my brain was very slow this morning, the answer wasn't coming to me fast. Picking up his keys, he said, "I'll be back with juice."

I guzzled some water; the coolness of it against my

dry throat felt so good. Without really raising my lips from the glass, I nodded and said, "Thanks, that'd be good." I was struggling, and forming words into sentences was too freaking hard; our conversation was going to be limited today but so far he didn't seem to care.

While he was gone, I contemplated trying to make myself look better. I even went so far as to drag myself into the bathroom and brush my hair and teeth. However, that was the extent of my effort. I had no doubt I'd regret this when I was feeling better.

Twenty minutes later he strode through my front door with bags of groceries and a determined look on his face.

"I thought you were just getting juice."

"Babe, you need more than juice," he stated as he handed me a banana, "Eat this, and then I've got some Gatorade for you to drink."

"I don't think I could stomach a banana, Scott."

"Eat it, it'll help get rid of your headache."

Oh, so bossy.

I watched him as I peeled the banana. He moved around my kitchen like it was his own, putting drinks in the fridge and adding more bananas to the fruit bowl. Not only had he bought me Gatorade and bananas, he'd also stocked me up on juice and coconut water.

"How the heck does a man like you know these things?" It could have just been my fried brain, but Scott didn't strike me as someone who would know what foods and drinks helped with sickness. There he was, dressed in jeans, big black boots, a tight black t-shirt, and his biker jacket. He had tattoos all over his arms and chunky silver rings on his fingers; he had that scary hot look about him. It was the kind of look that blazed a warning to me to stay away for the safety of my heart. Why, oh why, did God bring hot, sexy men into my life that were clearly not made for me?

He stopped what he was doing and gave me his full attention. "A man like me?" He crossed his arms in front of his chest while he waited for my reply.

"Well, you're a biker - " He raised his eyebrows. Shit, where were my freaking words today? "What I meant to say is, you don't come off as the type of man who would know that bloody bananas get rid of headaches." I was completely flustered now, and the banana would have no shot at clearing my headache because I'd just made it ten times worse.

"Yeah babe, I'm a biker but I'm not fucking ignorant. I do know things, for instance, that bananas help with hangovers."

I buried my head in my hands. This day had just started and I was already making a mess of it. Taking a deep breath, I looked up at him. "I'm sorry, I didn't mean to offend you."

"Takes a lot more than that to offend me. Now eat that banana. I've got shit to talk to you about and I need you thinking straight."

I did as I was told while racking my brain trying to

figure out what the heck he could want to talk to me about. He cleared the banana peels into the bin and brought me a Gatorade before sitting across from me at the table. I couldn't help staring at his arms as he folded them in front of him. Arms were it for me; the first thing I noticed about a guy, and I'd noticed Scott's that first day I'd met him. I quickly decided that he must spend a lot of time in the gym; he was built, and I bet if I were to reach out and touch him, he would be rock hard.

"My eyes are up here," he drawled, and when I lifted my eyes to his, I took in the sexy grin plastered on his face.

He knew how he was affecting me; no doubt he had the ladies lined up. Not being able to come up with a witty comeback, I did the only thing that came to mind. I poked my tongue at him. Yeah, real mature, but he did things to me; one of them being that he screwed with my mind and turned me into a hot mess, unable to process my thoughts quickly.

He surprised me by laughing. It was one of those genuine laughs that made his eyes crinkle, and that sent another jolt through me. Crinkled eyes were another turn on for me. Weird, I know, but there was just something about a man whose laughter touched his whole body. It was all tied up with my feelings about family, happiness and my desire to build a life with a man who also valued those things. Crinkled eyes symbolised those things to me.

I took a sip of Gatorade and waited for him to talk.

He indicated for me to drink more so I did. Finally he spoke. "The job's yours if you want it."

I nearly spat my drink all over him. "What? Why?" Again, sentences were not forthcoming.

"I was a dick to you last night. You were right; I don't know you. If you say you can handle asshole customers, I'll give you a shot."

Right. Dick last night. Asshole customers. Another shot. I churned through these thoughts much faster; the banana must be working. And then another thought occurred to me.

"How did you know where I live?"

"I asked Amy. You gave her your address last night to give to the cabbie. Now babe, focus, because I've got another appointment to get to. Do you want the job or not?"

"Are you always this bossy?"

"Yeah, it gets shit done."

"No, I meant with women. Do you boss every woman around that you meet?"

"I meet a lot of women, and yeah, I boss them around. But if you're asking whether I boss around the women whose homes I visit and who flash their ass at me on that visit, I couldn't tell you because I've never visited a woman at her home before."

There was that crinkle at his eyes again; the one that gave me butterflies in my stomach. He was watching me intently and it put me even more off my game.

"Well, just for the record, I've never flashed my ass at a man I just met. Not until today, anyway."

Oh, good Lord, his eyes crinkled even more if that was possible, and then he smiled which brought out his dimple, and I was completely gone. "I get that about you, babe. I've no doubt that if you weren't hungover, I wouldn't have been treated to any of what I've seen this morning."

Of course, just at a crucial moment in the conversation, my phone started ringing. It was where I'd left it last night, on the kitchen bench, and Scott stood up straight away to retrieve it. He grinned at me as he passed it to me. I wasn't sure why he was grinning like that so I ignored it and checked to see who was calling. Seeing that it was Cassie, my friend who took me out last night, I hit the button to silence the phone. She was a have-a-chat and would keep me on the phone for ages. Placing the phone on the table, I looked up to find Scott leaning against the bench with his arms folded, still grinning at me.

"What's so funny?" I asked.

"What the fuck is that song you've got for a ring tone?"

"Holding Out For A Hero by Bonnie Tyler. Why, what's wrong with it?" I asked, indignantly. I loved that song.

"How old is that song?"

"So I like songs from the eighties. I also love the nineties. You got something to say about that?"

He held up his hands in a defensive gesture. "Wouldn't dare, babe."

"Good. Now, about this job. I don't know what I was thinking last night. It must have been the alcohol. I don't want to work in a strip club, sorry. But thank you for making the effort to come here."

He nodded, and then pushed off from the bench. "That's what I figured, but thought I'd let you make that call." He checked his watch. "I've got to head."

I followed him down the hall, to the front door, making sure to check out his ass as I walked behind him. I figured I'd never get to see it again, so may as well enjoy it while I could. It was just my luck though, that he whipped around to face me just as he stepped outside, and caught the direction of my stare.

Chuckling again, he reminded me, "My eyes are up here."

Throwing caution to the wind, I muttered, "Yeah, but they're nowhere near as nice to look at." Holy shit, I couldn't believe I actually said that. I never flirted that openly with a man; usually I was too shy.

A slow smile formed across his face. "Never met anyone like you. You continue to surprise the shit outta me."

I smiled back. "Yeah, well I've never met anyone like you either."

"Later, sweetheart," he said, and left me standing there, drinking in the sexiness that was Scott Cole as he walked to his bike. My head still ached, although not as bad as earlier, and my stomach was still ill, but my happiness levels were at an all time high. It was just a damn shame that this was the last time I'd see him.

After Scott left, I spent a couple of hours lounging in front of the television, wishing for the time to pass quickly. The sooner I got through this day, the sooner I'd feel better. Mum rang me just after twelve o'clock to see how I was doing and to tell me that she picked up some more catering jobs. And then I remembered that Cassie had tried to call me earlier so I dialled her number.

She answered straight away. "Did you just wake up?" She sounded as awful as I felt.

"No, I was woken up by a visit from Scott earlier this morning."

"Scott, as in the guy from the club last night? The one who you met at the vet?"

"Yeah, him. He came to offer me a job, but I said no. I don't think I want to work in a strip club. Do you think I should have accepted it? We do need the money -"

"Stop second guessing yourself. And no, Harlow, I can't see you working in a strip club. We've known each other for what, six months now? You've become my best friend, and I need to tell you that it's time for you to chase your dreams now. You gave up everything to move here to help your Mum, and you did help her, but she's getting the café back on its feet now, so you should stop settling for any old job and go for what you want."

"I'm your best friend?" A warm sensation settled in my tummy.

"Yeah, you are," she replied, and I could hear the affection in her voice.

"You're mine too, girl."

"Oh my goodness, I feel like we just agreed to go steady, dude."

I laughed, but got serious when I said, "Cass, I haven't had a best friend for a long time now. Not since Dale cheated on me with Anna. He stole my best friend from me."

"No, they stole each other from you. She was just as much to blame as him, that bitch. Actually, I think what she did to you was worse. Best friends don't sleep with each other's boyfriends. First rule of best friend club."

"What's the second rule?" I teased her.

She was straight on it though. "Second rule is, if you hate someone, I hate them too. And third rule is, I've always got your back. You need me, you call me. I don't care what time of day it is. I live by that quote, it's the friends you can call at four am that matter."

"I think I love you even more than I loved you before I rang you. And I'm even feeling better too."

"Well, you just remember that. And don't forget that I'm a jealous bitch too."

Laughing, I said, "I know. I've seen you in action over Ben. God forbid any woman that makes a move on your man."

"Yeah, my husband knows how it is. And I feel the same way about you."

I sighed. "Seriously, Cass, you've made my day. You always manage to cheer me up when I'm feeling down."

"That's what I'm here for. Now, back to your job situation. I know you've always wanted to pursue your art, and you're a damn good artist so I think you should look into ways to get your art out there."

"I don't think it's something that can earn me a living."

"You won't know unless you try though, will you?"

"Mmmm…"

"Mmmm's your way of fobbing me off, and I'm not letting you do that this time. We need to get your paintings into a gallery."

"Oh, God, you're taking over, aren't you?" Memories of the time that Cassie had harassed a car dealer into selling a car to me for less than he wanted to came to mind.

"Think of it as me being your manager. Christ, I need something to keep me occupied while Ben has me stuck at home being his Stepford wife."

"You're the farthest thing from a freaking Stepford wife. Ben could only hope for you to be submissive but we all know that you wear the pants in that relationship."

"Okay, okay, you're right. Anyway, leave it with me; I'll get you into a gallery. You just start painting."

I could hear the excitement in her voice. Cassie loved a mission. "It's all yours, but I may need to get a part time job in the meantime."

"Do what you've gotta do, but like I said, get painting."

"Yes, boss," I promised, and we finished our conversation.

I spent the next few hours pampering myself, hoping it would negate the effects of the hangover. I showered and gave myself a facial, pedicure and manicure. At the end of it all, I felt a million times better. So, it was on that high that I received a phone call from my mum that shot all my plans to shit.

"Harlow, honey, one of the fridges at the café died. I'm rushing around trying to sort all the food into the other fridge, but I'm pretty busy and could do with a hand serving customers while I take care of it." She sounded frazzled.

"Sure, Mum. Give me ten minutes, and I'll be there."

"You're a lifesaver. Thank you," she replied, and hung up.

I quickly threw on a dress, grabbed my keys and bag, and drove the short distance to Mum's café. We lived about six minutes from it, which I loved because traffic and I didn't see eye to eye. There were way too many idiots on the road, and too many road rules to follow.

Mum's body sagged a little when she saw me walk through the front door. The tension just whooshed out of her. Being such a strong, independent woman since the day my father died when I was fifteen, she had a tendency to take everything on by herself and hated to ask for help.

"Thanks for coming," she greeted me, and gave me a hug.

I grabbed an apron and shooed her with my hands, "Go. Sort your fridges. I'll take care of the customers."

She saluted me. "Yes, honey. I'm gone." And with that, she darted out to the back kitchen.

I spent the next few hours making coffees and serving food. It was a fairly busy afternoon, and the time flew by. Mum dealt with her fridge storage issues and then made calls to find out about getting the fridge fixed. Just after five thirty she appeared at the counter looking upset. I'd just locked the front door after seeing the last customer out.

"What's wrong?" I asked her with a sinking feeling.

Mum was such a practical person; not much made her look that down.

"I need a new fridge and that's going to cost thousands. Thousands that I don't have."

"Shit."

She exhaled loudly. "Just when things were turning around. Why is it always two steps forward and five steps back? For once, I just want things to be easy."

I went to her and grabbed her in a huge hug. "We'll work it out, Ma. We always do."

She clung to me for a few minutes and then pulled away, exhausted eyes searching mine. "I'm not sure how this time, Harlow. It feels like we're at the end of our rope. And I'm not sure I have it in me to fight anymore. I'm sick of rolling with the punches. I'm black and blue from them."

My heart cracked a little more for her. She'd done so much for me in my life; made so many sacrifices. It was my turn now to do that for her. And I knew I had at least one option open to me.

"I'll help. I think I can get a night job and that will help pay for the fridge. But I need to go there now before they give the job to someone else. Will you be okay to close up by yourself?"

She nodded, relief flooding her face. "Thank you," she almost whispered, and I could tell she was fighting tears.

"I love you, Mum. And I'll do anything to make this work."

"I love you too, baby girl. You're the best thing that ever happened to me."

I left her to close up, and flew down Sandgate Road towards the Valley. Our café was at Clayfield and Scott's club was in the Valley. Unfortunately, it was bloody peak hour so traffic was a bitch. What would normally take me ten minutes, took me just over twenty. Between that trip and finding a park when I got there, I'd managed to yell abuse at one driver and give another the finger. As I walked to the club from the carpark, I contemplated the intelligence of my decision to give up smoking a year ago. I could really do with a cigarette right about now.

When I got to the front door it was locked. Damn it. I probably should have realised they wouldn't be open at six o'clock at night. Digging in my bag, I found my phone and Googled their phone number. No answer. Shit. I dialed it again, hoping to annoy them into answering but still no answer.

"Can I help you?" a deep voice surprised me from behind. I spun around and was met with the greenest eyes I think I'd ever seen.

"Do you work here?"

"Who's asking?"

I stepped back and ran my gaze over him. He was tall and dressed in similar clothes to what Scott had been wearing the last time I saw him; jeans, black t-shirt, biker vest and boots. He didn't appear to have any tattoos but he was rocking the chunky rings; just about every finger had a ring on it. And he was stacked with muscles. He ran his fingers through his dark hair, and the corded muscles in his arms screamed at me for attention.

"My name's Harlow, and I'm looking for Scott. Scott Cole; do you know him?"

Nodding, he sized me up. He must have decided I was okay because he stepped around me and unlocked the front door, ushering me in. I entered and got a good look at the club as it was lit up. Oh, good Lord, that carpet. It was worse than the carpet you saw in an RSL club; gaudy as hell. But I figured that no-one would be paying much attention to it and besides, the lights were usually off during business hours. Red seemed to be the main colour of Indigo; red carpet splashed with little black symbols, red walls, and red seats that had a touch of black on them. There was a circular bar area a little off centre to the right as you entered the room, and the stage where I was guessing the strippers did their thing was to the left.

I followed the guy past the bar, around to the right, and through a locked door. Now we were in a short hallway that we followed to the end, at which point he stopped and knocked on the door we were now standing in front of.

"Scott, you free? I've got a Harlow here to see you."

I waited quietly, watching the guy and wondering about him. There was something about him; something that told me not to screw with him. He had the look and the aura of a man that you wouldn't want to meet in a dark alley.

My thoughts were interrupted when the door flung open and Scott appeared, looking a little tense. He frowned when he saw me. "What's wrong?"

I was quick to reassure him because he really did look worried. "Nothing's wrong. I just came to ask you something."

That seemed to placate him; the tension eased off his face and his shoulders relaxed a little. "Sure," he said, and moved aside to let me into his office. Nodding at the guy, he said, "Thanks, Griff. Can you make sure Amy's stocked the fridge at the bar?"

Griff nodded slowly, his attention still on me. It was disconcerting; almost like he was sizing me up, trying to work out if I was the enemy. I had no idea what that was about. Finally, he made a move to leave. "Will do."

After he'd left, Scott turned to me. "Out with it, babe. What do you need?"

"I need that job if it's still going." My tummy was full of butterflies and I wasn't sure if I was nervous about asking for the job or whether just being around Scott was affecting me.

"I thought you didn't want to work in a strip club."

Moment of truth. I decided to be honest; I figured Scott was the type to appreciate full disclosure. "I'll be honest, I don't really want to. However, I need to; to help support my mother and I."

"Sit," he ordered me, and pointed to a couch against the wall.

I did as I was told, and he leant against his desk, crossing his feet. He wrapped one arm around his torso while the other one balanced on it, his hand supporting his chin.

"Is your mother sick?"

"No. She runs her own café and times have been tough. That's why I moved back to Brisbane; to help her keep it afloat and help pay her mortgage. Things were looking up, and they still are, but one of her fridges died today and she needs a new one, which is going to cost her a fair bit of money."

He nodded. "Right. So now you need this job to help pay for that," he stated, deep in thought.

"Yes."

I waited while he continued to mull it over, although I wasn't sure what he had to think about; either he had a job for me or he didn't. Eventually he pushed off from the desk and walked around to the other side and sat. He picked up his phone and dialed a number. His eyes landed on me while he waited for the person to answer; they were serious, with no crinkle.

The person finally answered, and he spoke, "Hey, brother, I need a fridge for a cafe. Not sure exactly what yet, but you able to help me out?"

I struggled to maintain my composure. He was getting me a fridge? I just wanted a job.

Scott continued to discuss fridges with the person on

the other end of the phone and then he hung up. "That's sorted, babe. Tomorrow I'll call you to get the info on the fridge you need and it'll be delivered tomorrow afternoon."

"Umm… I don't think my Mum has the money to pay for it yet. The idea was for me to get this job and we'd save for a new fridge."

"You can't run a café without a fridge. We'll get that sorted first. You can have the job here and we can discuss you paying for the fridge later." His tone was clear; this is how it would be, and don't argue with me.

"No, I'll work here and save, and then get the fridge. We can't ask that of you."

"You didn't. But you're getting it anyway." Before I could argue anymore, another guy appeared at the door. Holy heck, did God rain hot, sexy men down into this club? This guy was smoking. Upon closer inspection, I realised it was Madison's boyfriend, J. I'd met him at the barbeque but I hadn't really paid much attention to him as I was focusing more on Scott.

He had his phone in his hand and looked stressed. "Scott, Madison's on the phone. She says the cat really wants that fucking collar off and won't shut up about it. I've got shit I'm supposed to be taking care of and the last fucking thing I need is her on my ass about your cat." He held his phone out to Scott. "Talk to her and sort this shit out, brother."

Scott scowled at him, but took the phone. "Jesus, Madison, it's a fucking cat for Christ's sake. Deal with it. I'll be over in a couple of hours to get him." He looked at me, and then said to her, "Hang on a minute."

Moving the phone away from his mouth, he asked me, "Can she take the collar off the cat?"

I figured they were talking about Monty. "No, don't take it off because he'll scratch his wound and it could get infected. And then you'll be up for more money." I was a little confused as to why Madison had Monty.

He mouthed thanks at me, and then moved the phone back in place, "Whatever you fucking do, don't take that collar off the cat. He's already cost me a fortune."

Ending his conversation, he hung up and gave the phone back to the guy, who took one last look at me and then left us alone.

"Do you always talk to people like that? And why does Madison have Monty?" I asked.

"Like what?"

"You were so rude to her."

"Madison can be a pain in the ass."

I stood up, and smoothed my dress down, not failing to notice Scott checking out my legs. I could thank the running I did for that.

"Where I come from, we would never talk to our sister that way."

"And where's that?" he asked as he stood and walked around the desk.

"Gympie."

"You're straight up country, aren't you?"

"What does *that* mean?"

He chuckled. "Just making an observation. It's refreshing actually."

I had no idea what he meant by that so I ignored it. "You never answered me. Why does Madison have Monty?"

"Couldn't trust Michelle with him so I asked Madison to look after him for awhile. She loves cats."

As he said this, he moved so he was next to me and put his hand on my arm to guide me out of the office. Locking the door behind him, he then ushered me down the hall and back into the club. Being this close to him was intoxicating, and his touch sent a thrill through me. It was a good thing that he'd stopped talking to me because only gibberish would have come out of my mouth in reply.

I followed him to the bar where he stopped and faced me.

"You ever worked a bar before?"

Nodding, I said, "Yeah, I know how to pour a beer."

"Thank fuck for that." He motioned to the girl behind the bar to get her attention. I recognised her from the other night. "Amy, Harlow's going to be starting tomorrow night. She's got experience but I'll need you to show her the ropes."

"Sure," Amy agreed, and smiled at me.

Scott turned to me. "That work for you?"

"Yes, thank you."

He gave me one short nod. "Good. I'll leave you to

chat with Amy about what to wear and when to arrive. I've got to go."

"Okay. And again, thank you for the job."

He'd already started to walk away, but he looked back at me and said, "Don't forget to call me first thing in the morning with that fridge info."

"Right, will do."

He exited out the front door of the club, and I wondered just what I'd gotten myself into. Sure I'd done bar work before, but never in a strip club. And besides all that, I'd be working for Scott Cole, and I really wasn't sure how I felt about that.

10

W *hat the fuck had I just agreed to?*

Harlow was sweet as fucking pie. I wasn't sure she'd cut it at Indigo, and yet I'd said yes to her working there. Christ, I was thinking with my dick. And speaking of my dick, I really needed to get laid; it'd been over a week since I'd seen any pussy and that was a week too fucking long.

"Scott, where the fuck have you been?"

I eyed my father; my thoughts interrupted. He was sitting with Griff and J at a table in the corner of the clubhouse bar, waiting for me, and appeared to be irritated.

I grabbed a chair and turned it around so that I was sitting with its back to my front. "Hiring staff for Indigo," I snapped at him.

"Good. That's one headache gone. And it looks like

the situation with Blade and Bullet might have resolved itself too."

My skepticism kicked in. "Really?"

Dad looked really pissed off with me now. "Why the fuck can't you get past your issues with Blade?"

"I don't trust him. Not sure I ever will. So when you say that he's suddenly agreed to pull back on his plans to move more coke, I don't buy it."

"He's given me his word."

I snorted. "His word means nothing to me. I think we need to still be on guard for shit to go down between him and Black Deeds."

Dad slammed his hand down on the table; he was wearing his anger. "Been the President of Storm for a long fucking time, son. I'm always on fucking guard so don't tell me how to do that part of my job. It's fucking insulting. As for Blade, I don't want to hear another fucking word from you about him. He's my son and when he gives me his word, I trust it."

I glared at him, seething at his words. My relationship with my father was completely fucked to the point that I hated him now; hated what he'd done to my mother and hated that he'd had a whole other family. What kind of man did that to his wife and kids? Obviously the kind of man that I didn't know quite as well as I thought I did.

"Griff, can I see you in my office? Got some paperwork I need you to look at," he said and left with Griff.

J blew out a breath. "I fucking hate your old man."

"You're not the only one, brother," I said as I shoved my hand through my hair.

We sat in silence for a moment, contemplating that, but J was like me and hated going over and over shit so he moved on to another subject quickly. "Hey, what's with the blonde you hired? Saw the way you looked at her."

"How the fuck did I look at her?"

He smirked. "Hate to break it to you, but I've never seen you look at a woman that way before."

I leant forward and demanded, "What fucking way, J?"

"Like you want to fuck her and not let her go, brother."

I shoved my chair back. Standing, I muttered, "Not fucking likely. Told you before, that shit's not for me."

J laughed. "We'll see."

I left him there, laughing to himself. He had me thinking about Harlow though. And that pissed me off because I had so many other things I should be thinking about. This was one reason why I didn't want to settle down. I'd watched friends settle down; it fucking consumed them and I didn't have the time or desire for that.

THE NEXT MORNING, I still hadn't heard from Harlow at eleven o'clock so I picked up the phone and called her.

"Sorry, I've been so busy that I haven't had time to scratch myself," she answered the phone in a flap. It brought a smile to my face; couldn't tell you why, but it did.

"All good. But I need the fridge details so I can get that organised for you."

"I've got a line that's six customers deep. Can I text you the info once I get through them?"

"Sure. And once I know what's happening, I'll let you know," I said and hung up. I put the phone down and leant back in my seat thinking about her. I'd actually been thinking about her all last night and most of this morning. Fuck, I'd been waiting for her call. Not my finest moment; waiting for a woman to call me. I wasn't sure what it was about Harlow that put her in my thoughts so often but I suspected it was how different she was to every other woman I'd ever met. Being VP of Storm, I'd had my share of women who just wanted in on the club. They were an easy lay; there was no challenge there. In fact, there was never any challenge from any of them. Harlow was the opposite; she'd questioned me repeatedly. It annoyed the shit out of me, and yet, at the same time, it turned me the fuck on. I wanted more of her sassy mouth.

AT THREE O'CLOCK I parked my bike outside her café. I'd organised the fridge delivery and even though there was no need for me to be, I found myself here for it. I stood outside for a couple of minutes assessing the outside of the café. The outside needed some work; a lick of paint and some new signs wouldn't go astray. I pushed through the front door and was hit by the country feel they had going on; red and white checkered tablecloths and other random country knick knacks were impossible to miss. It seemed out of place in the middle of Brisbane.

My eyes landed on Harlow who was bending over sweeping dirt up. Fuck, she had an amazing ass and I couldn't pull my gaze away. I planted my feet wide and crossed my arms across my chest, enjoying the view. She was wearing those tight jeans again and when she finally stood up straight and turned around, I sucked in a breath at the tight as sin red strapless top she had on. Christ, my dick jerked to attention at that.

She was momentarily caught off guard by my presence but quickly recovered, throwing a smile in my direction. "What are you doing here?"

"Came to make sure the fridge arrives okay."

"Thanks, I appreciate that." She walked away from me, towards the counter, and my eyes were trained to her ass again.

The sound of kids coming through the front door pulled me away from what I was doing. Harlow's face lit up and she greeted the kids. "Hey, you two! Time for some red velvet cake?"

Their mother laughed and nodded. "Yeah, they've been hanging out to come and see you and also to have some cake. But mostly to see you."

Harlow indicated to a seat in the front window. "Take a seat and I'll bring cake and milkshakes for you." She looked at me, her face flushed with delight, and said, "Do you want some cake while you wait?"

Not what I'd been expecting but fuck, I never knocked cake back. "Sure, thanks."

She flashed me a brilliant smile and said, "Great! Grab a seat, I won't be long."

I did what she said and waited for my cake while I watched her interact with the kids. She was a natural with them and I found myself wondering why Lisa couldn't have been blessed with a mother like her; a woman who genuinely loved being with children and gave them her full attention. While I was waiting, an older woman came out from the back area. She looked so much like Harlow that I knew she had to be her mother.

She came over to where I was sitting. "You must be Scott." She smiled at me.

"I am. What was the dead giveaway?"

Now she laughed. "Could have been the tattoos, or the boots but it was probably the cut you're wearing." She winked at me. I liked this woman straight away and that was something that rarely happened.

"Harlow hasn't told me your name."

She extended her hand and shook mine. "I'm Cheryl. Nice to meet you. And thank you for what you've done for me with the fridge."

"Good to meet you too, Cheryl. As I said to Harlow, you can't run a café without the right equipment. Happy to help where I can."

Harlow interrupted us at that moment when she called across the room. "Mum, can you get Scott some red velvet cake please?"

Cheryl smiled and nodded. "Absolutely. You want a coffee too? Or another drink?"

"Coffee would be good, thanks."

"Coming right up," she promised and left to go and make it.

I sat watching Harlow again after her mother left and didn't realise that the time had passed when Cheryl came back to the table with cake and coffee. She actually had two coffees in her hand, and when she sat at the table with me, I realised she was settling in for a chat.

"Why do I get the impression this is going to be a heart to heart?"

"You're a very intuitive man, Scott. And you're a man who my daughter hasn't stopped talking about for the past couple of days so I want to take this opportunity to find out why."

I raised my eyebrows. Fuck, this woman was direct;

another thing I liked about her. "What do you want to know?"

"The thing I want to know about you isn't something I'm going to discover from a conversation over coffee. I just wanted to sit with you for a bit and get a feel for you."

"You don't pull any punches do you?"

"No, but especially not when it comes to Harlow. She's been screwed over too many times in life and I don't want to see that happen to her again."

"Fair enough. I have to tell you though, that there's nothing between me and Harlow, so you can rest easy."

"See, I would have believed that if you hadn't shown up here today. I would have believed it was all on Harlow's end but you turning up to oversee a fridge delivery that didn't need overseeing, that tells me a lot." She drank some of her coffee and pointed at my cake. "Eat up, it's good."

This woman had managed to do something that most people couldn't do; she'd stunned me into silence. So, I ate cake. It was the safer option. And fuck, it was good cake.

Smiling, she said, "Harlow's a good cook. Would you agree?"

"Did Harlow make this?"

She nodded. "Yes, it's her favourite cake."

Damn, it was now my favourite cake too. It was fucking delicious; the best cake I'd ever had. We sat in silence, eating cake and drinking coffee until Harlow joined us a couple of minutes later.

"How was the cake?" she asked looking at my empty plate.

"Was just about to tell your Mum that it's the best cake I've ever had."

She fucking blushed. And then she gave me another of her mega watt smiles and I decided right then and fucking there that Harlow was a risk to my manhood. I wanted her in a way I'd never wanted a woman. I needed to get my shit together and get laid; that would fix the problem.

Before she could open her mouth and do further damage the front door opened and two delivery guys walked in. I stood and tipped my chin to them. "You here with a fridge?"

"Yeah, mate. Where do you want it?"

I nodded at Cheryl. "Ask the boss."

I drowned out the noise of their conversation as they worked out where the fridge was going and instead focused on Harlow as she cleaned away the cake and coffee dishes. She went out the back somewhere and when she didn't return, I wandered out there looking for her. She was loading the dishwasher in the kitchen and I leaned against the doorframe, watching her quietly.

She knew I was there because without stopping what she was doing she said, "Thank you so much for getting us a fridge. My Mum really appreciates it."

"Your Mum is something else."

She finished with the dishwasher and closed it before turning to look at me. My eyes dropped to her chest. That top fit her tits like a glove; any man would struggle to keep their eyes off her chest. I wasn't a saint and had no problem showing my appreciation so it took me more than a few moments to look back up to her face. She was shaking her head at me but there was a hint of a smile.

I smirked. "Sweetheart, if you're gonna wear shit like that you've gotta expect men to stare."

"Turn around."

"What?"

She repeated herself. "I said, turn around."

"Yeah, I got that but I'm wondering where you're going with this."

She walked over to me until she was in my personal space. A sexy smile came over her face and she said, "I want you to turn around so that I can check out your ass cause baby, a woman's got needs and if you're gonna wear shit like that, her needs are gonna be fulfilled."

I reached out and curled my hand around her neck, pulling her closer. "Fuck woman, what are doing to me?"

Her breathing became ragged. "The same thing you're doing to me."

Our eyes searched each other's and I was just about to kiss her when Cheryl interrupted us. "Scott, the delivery guys need a hand with the fridge."

Without taking my eyes off Harlow, I replied, "Be there in a minute."

She left and instead of moving straight away, I held my hand steady on her neck. "This conversation isn't finished; not by a long fucking shot."

Harlow didn't say a word; she just nodded. Reluctantly, I let go of her neck and left her to go and help with the fridge.

I held up the red leather dress and assessed it again. Bloody hell, I'd never fit in this tiny thing. And if I did, it was going to stick to me like cling wrap.

Amy laughed and I landed desperate eyes on her. "Do I really have to wear this?"

"Yes, you do. But we all do so you won't be the odd one out."

I blew out a breath. "Okay, give me a minute to put it on and then I'll be out so you can show me around."

She nodded and left me to it. I was staring my first shift at Indigo in the eyes and to say I was nervous was an understatement. After quickly undressing, I wiggled my way into the red outfit. Holy heck, it was the tightest and shortest thing I think I'd ever worn. I surveyed myself in the mirror. The dress was low cut so my cleavage was on display, and turning slightly, I noted how it hugged my ass. Thank God I kept myself in shape. I didn't look too bad but I was a little self conscious. However, I put on my big girl panties and dealt with it; this was for my Mum and she'd given me everything in life so this was the least I could do in return.

A couple of minutes later I was out the front and Amy started showing me how they ran things at Indigo. I'd worked quite a few bar jobs in my time and I was pretty impressed with the smoothness of this operation; they had it fine tuned.

We spent a good half hour going over procedures before Amy surprised me by saying, "Scott shocked me when he hired you."

I took in her serious face. "Why's that?"

"Well he didn't interview you and when I asked him about that, he got shitty with me for asking. He also didn't get Griff to check you out; another standard procedure for him. But the strangest thing is that you pissed him off the other night when you were in here drunk and I've never seen someone get the time of day from Scott again after they piss him off like that. Not unless it's his sister or a Storm member. People only have one chance with Scott."

Wow. And she didn't know that I'd upset him on more than one occasion now. I tried to play it off. "I guess I'd better not piss him off again, huh?"

She smiled at me now; just a small smile, but one nonetheless. "Oh, I think you're good to go, Harlow.

From what I've seen it looks like you could get away with it."

I felt heat rise to my face. "Bloody men. He just brings it out in me; I don't mean to argue with him."

"Story of my life too. My hubby has this way of pushing all my buttons until I lose my shit at him. The make-up sex is off the charts though," she said, winking at me.

I laughed and felt like we'd bonded a little. It was a good start to a new job; there was nothing worse than starting a new job and not getting along with your new workmates.

She checked the time. "Okay, we have about half an hour till opening time. Let's go over a couple more things."

FOUR HOURS LATER, I was sitting in the staff room on my break. So far, I'd enjoyed the shift. For the most part the customers weren't too bad. They really only had eyes for the strippers anyway so they didn't ogle me too much. Well not anymore than the average man in the street. What had taken me by surprise a little was the number of women customers; not the ones who were there with their men but rather the ones who were there to check out the strippers. I shouldn't have been surprised but I was.

My break was almost over when Scott walked in. I

was standing in front of the locker that each staff member had and turned when I heard him. He stopped abruptly and took in my appearance.

"Fuck," he muttered and shook his head.

"What?" *Geez, what had I done now*? I placed my hands on my hips in a defensive stance while I waited for his answer.

He stalked over to where I was standing, and resting his arm on the locker above my head, he leant into me. I was intoxicated by his scent of leather and oil, and butterflies scattered in my tummy. "You've got no fuckin' idea, have you?"

Hell, with him this close to me, I had no freaking idea about anything. My mind was completely lost to him at this moment. "Scott, can you give me a hint, because I'm drawing a blank at the moment."

"Jesus," he said and then stopped himself, pushing off from the locker and away from me. He took a step back, eyes burning into me, and then said, "Fuck."

Now I was really confused but before I could say another word, he turned and stalked out of the room. I was left standing in a daze. *What the hell*?

Without thinking, I took off after him. I found him in his office; he'd just walked in and still had his back to me. "What was that?" I demanded.

He turned to look at me. "That was me walking away before I did something we'd both regret."

I crinkled my forehead; he wasn't making sense to me. "Why would we regret it?"

"Shit, Harlow, we're completely different people from different worlds, for one. And two, if something was to happen between us, it would be a one off for me and I'm fairly certain it wouldn't be that for you."

How dare he presume to know what I wanted. "So you get to make these decisions based on presumptions you've made? Without asking me what I actually want? You really are a throwback to previous generations, aren't you?"

Anger blazed in his eyes. "What the fuck does that mean?"

"It means that women have come a long bloody way in the past couple of decades, Mr. Caveman. We're quite capable of choosing what we want these days, and in case you missed it, we also don't mind one off sex every now and then."

"Babe, I've not met a woman yet who can do one night stands. They always want more and I've got nothing more to give."

"Well, maybe you should try me. I don't want the bullshit lies and excuses that men come up with after they promise you the world and then fail to deliver. One night, with no promises sounds like my kind of night."

He cocked an eyebrow. "I'm not buying it, sweetheart. You're too much of a nice girl."

Bloody hell, I was sick of men dumping me in that category! I'd show him nice. I flicked my hair and plastered a sweet smile on my face. Walking towards him, I stopped when I reached him. "You ever had nice,

Scott? Cause I'm betting you haven't. And in that case, you've got no idea what you're missing because nice is sweet and sweet hits the spot. Every. Fucking. Time," I purred and then shrugged, "It's a damn shame that you're not into nice. But that's okay, because I bet Nash would be." I winked at him as I said that last bit and then walked out of the room. I had to get back to my shift but I also wanted to get as far from Scott as possible; I didn't handle rejection very well. Especially not after I'd practically thrown myself at a man.

THE REST of my shift went well. I didn't see Scott again which was a blessing; I needed some time to get my shit together before I saw him again.

"You did good tonight, girl," Amy smiled at me as she gave me a compliment.

"Thanks, Amy, that means a lot."

"You coming back for some more tonight?"

"I'm not sure when Scott wants me to work again but I hope so because I need the money."

"Well, we're down staff so I reckon you'll be called in for tonight."

"Great." I followed her and our security guy outside. There a rule that he was to escort all the staff to their cars at the end of their shift. Amy took off to her car and I headed towards mine. I was stunned to see Scott leaning against it, arms crossed over his chest, and one foot casually crossed over the other. He nodded at the security guy who then left us alone. I just stood rooted to the spot, not sure what to do or say.

He slowly pushed off from the car and uncrossed his arms. "You're right. I've never had nice," he said gruffly.

I was still slightly annoyed at him. "Well, I can highly recommend it, and I'm sure I could suggest some places to go looking for it."

"Don't push me, Harlow. I'm trying to apologise here," he warned me in that low, gravelly voice that threatened to melt my panties. Damn.

"You say that like I should be thankful for your apology; like I should worship at your feet for it." I knew I was perhaps being a little snarky but, bloody hell, I'd had enough of men who thought I owed them something just for them being nice to me. From now on, I would be an equal in a relationship or I wouldn't be in the relationship at all.

He grabbed my arm and roughly pulled me to him. "I don't apologise to people. Ever."

"Well, bully for you," I said and pushed against his chest to try and put some space between us but he held on to me, keeping me close.

"Fuck, woman. Are you always this much work?"

I stopped trying to get away from him and glared at him. "I may have told you that I wanted one night with you but I didn't mean I would be an easy lay. You'd have to work for it because I have high standards these days."

"I can deal with high standards, babe, but I need some give and take. When I'm trying to fix something I've said or done wrong, I need you to work with me rather than stay in your pissy mood and prolong the whole fucking thing."

"You really have a way of making something you've said sound wrong when actually it was the right thing to say, don't you?"

"I just say it like it is. People can take it or leave it; I don't give a fuck."

God, he was exasperating and hot all at the same time. It was seriously doing my head in. "And what would you say if I said I wanted to leave it?"

"I'd tell you to stop fucking around."

"So, in other words, you do give a fuck where I'm concerned." I was starting to enjoy this conversation.

He scowled. "Don't twist my words."

I smiled innocently at him. "I'm not really twisting them, but it is fun to point out the obvious to you."

He blew out a breath and then muttered, "Just get in the car." He wasn't pointing at my car though; he was pointing at the Charger parked next to mine.

"That's not my car."

"I know, babe. It's mine."

"Why would I be getting in your car?"

"Because I'm driving you home in it." He'd

unlocked and opened my door and was gesturing for me to get in.

Oh, good Lord! "I'm quite capable of driving myself home, Scott."

"Yeah, well I'm driving you home so just get in the damn car." He looked shitty with me again.

My natural reaction was to continue to argue with him but I quickly assessed the situation and decided it'd just be easier if I got in the car and let him drive me home. "Fine, but what about my car? Will it be safe here?"

He nodded and put his hand out. "Give me your keys. Griff's gonna drive your car to your house and then I'll bring him back here."

"You're not kidding are you?" It seemed like a lot of effort to go to.

"I don't kid," he said and looked towards Griff who was walking our way.

I shook my head, reached in my bag for my keys and handed them over. Then, I got in his car and shut up. I thought it really was the only thing to do at that point.

"I told you I don't trust that motherfucker."

Griff held up his hand to stop me. "All I told you was that they were Blade's boys. We don't know if he's sent them or if they came on their own."

"Don't give me that shit, Griff. Of course he fuckin' sent them. And now Harlow's in the middle of all this."

"We'll keep her out of it."

"Bullshit. You saw them watching her last night."

"Maybe they were just checking her out rather than watching her for Blade."

I scoffed. "No, they'd been sent to trail her. What I want to know is, why?"

J walked into the office and sat down, leaning back with his hands raised behind his head. "Heard that Harlow's being targeted. That true?"

"Fuck," Griff muttered. "We don't know for sure yet but we're taking precautions and looking into it."

"Since when?" J asked.

"We noticed last night when she was working at Indigo that there were some guys watching her. Griff looked back over the surveillance and confirmed they'd been there watching all night. I drove her home and we kept watch on her house with Stoney taking over early this morning. We're keeping someone on her until we figure out what's going on," I answered him.

"You want me to take over from Stoney for awhile?"

"Yeah, sounds good. I'll leave that with you and then can you organise Nash to take over from you so we can do those interviews this afternoon?"

J nodded in agreement and then left.

"You got Harlow working at Indigo tonight?" Griff asked.

"Yeah, and I'll be in to keep an eye out. Today you and I are going to try and find out what the fuck's going on."

"One step ahead of you. I've already put a tail on those two assholes who were at Indigo last night."

"I've got half a mind just to pay Blade a visit."

"Not yet, Scott. Let's do a little quiet investigating first." Griff was right but my natural instinct was to go in guns blazing so I had to restrain myself.

I WAS in the office when Harlow arrived for her shift that night. I knew she was here because Nash informed me after tailing her to the club; not because she came and saw me. She'd been pissy that I'd insisted on driving her home last night and I hadn't enlightened her as to the reason why I'd wanted to do it so I presumed she was still shitty over that.

A couple of hours passed by before I left the office to go in search of her. Nash had kept watch while I finished up paperwork and other admin shit that had to be done. As I walked into the club area he nodded at me and left; apparently he had a chick waiting for him somewhere. I eyed Harlow and sucked in a breath at the sight of her. Christ, she looked fucking amazing tonight. The red dress was in place, her blonde hair was out and her face was flushed with a huge smile in place. She leant across the bar so she could hear what a customer was saying to her and when she threw her head back and laughed at whatever it was that he said, a shot of jealousy ran through me.

Fuck.

Some form of instinct took over and I stalked over to the bar. "Harlow," I barked, and when she whipped her head around in surprise, I continued, "My office. Now."

She raised her eyebrows but did as I said. I followed close behind, my eyes glued to her ass that was barely covered by the damn dress we made our Indigo girls wear. When we got to the office, she walked in, turned around and crossed her arms in front of her.

"What?" she snapped.

"How's your shift going?"

"Surely you didn't call me away from work to ask me that?"

Christ, what the hell was I doing?

I sighed and rubbed my chin. "Can we start over here? I've managed to piss you off without even fuckin' meaning to."

It took a moment but her gaze softened. "Okay."

"Clean slate, yeah?"

Nodding, she said, "Yes, clean slate." The tension had seeped out of her.

"Right, let's start with the caveman allegations. Not completely true but, I've got reasons for everything I do. Your mother mentioned that you'd been screwed over before, and I respect you enough to not want to fuck with you. That was the only reason why I said it'd be a bad idea for us to sleep together. Not because I was taking the decision out of your hands. Fuck, trust me babe when I say that I want a taste of your pussy, but for once in my life I'm not being a selfish prick. As for driving you home, there's some fuckers out there at that time of night and I wanted to make sure you got home okay." I paused for a moment and moved so I was close enough to smell her scent that drove my dick wild. My voice dropped to a low rumble. "And as for Nash wanting a piece of your nice? That motherfucker isn't getting close enough to you ever again. You read me, babe?"

Her chest rose and fell rapidly as her breathing picked up and a smile touched her face. "I read you. On all of it. Now, do you want me to get back to work?"

"Yeah, but that dress is gonna be a problem for me."

"Ah, I hate to break it to you big boy, but it's the only option." She was grinning that sexy fucking grin at me that made me want to rip that fucking dress off here and now.

"Yeah, I know. I fucking know," I muttered.

She laughed and it was the sweetest fucking sound. *Jesus. Where were these thoughts coming from?* I flicked my hand towards the door. "Go. And Harlow, I'm driving you home again tonight."

She rolled her eyes, but simply said, "Yes, Scott." And then she was gone and I was left wondering yet again, what the fuck I was doing.

13

I sat at a table and laid my head down, closing my eyes for a minute. After only four hours sleep, I was exhausted. Working at Indigo at night and here during the day was going to kill me eventually. Mum had told me not to come in until later but I knew she had cakes to make for orders so I didn't want to leave her on her own to do that and serve customers. Thank goodness I had tonight off work from Indigo; me and my bed were going to get very cozy together.

"Harlow, wake up." Someone was gently shaking my shoulders. I cocked one eye open and peered out to see who it was.

"Go away, Madison," I grumbled, not really meaning it, "Your brother has worn me out and I need sleep."

She smirked. "I knew he had a thing for you. How long you two been going at it?"

I snapped my head up. "Oh no, you misunderstood. Crap, I guess I did put it kinda like that, didn't I? No, nothing's happening between us -"

She cut me off. "Slow down, honey. Deep breath."

I did as she suggested and took a very long, deep breath. "I've been working at Indigo the last two nights and the café during the days so I'm pretty tired. That's all I meant."

She dumped her bag on the table and sat across from me. "Yeah, I heard you were working at Indigo. I feel so out of the loop with all your news; I haven't had time to come in for my coffee the last few days. Why did you take a job there and how did you know that Scott was looking for staff? I'm still trying to wrap my head around it all because you and Scott didn't really hit it off at the barbeque."

"You want a coffee for this?"

"Girl, you know me too well. Of course I want a coffee."

I smiled and then hopped up to go and get her coffee. "We need to hang out more often," I said as I made it.

"Yes! How about next Friday night? I've become friends with my hairdresser and she and I are having a girl's night out."

"Count me in, so long as I'm not working at Indigo. I need a girl's night out. Can I bring a friend?"

She nodded enthusiastically. "Hell yes, the more the merrier."

I made us both a coffee and then settled back in across from her. "Long story as to why I'm working at Indigo, but basically just what I told you last week; I need the money to help Mum with her bills. One of her fridges died on Tuesday and we couldn't afford to replace it so I asked Scott for the job. And, he also organised a fridge for us. Oh, and this was after I turned up at his club drunk and abused him for losing me my job at the vet's."

"Wait. How did you know Indigo was his club?"

I shook my head. "I didn't. My friend and I were out drowning my sorrows about losing my job and we saw Indigo and wondered what a strip club looked like on the inside. So, we went in. The rest is history."

She was laughing. "You'd never been inside a strip club before?"

"No! I'm a good, country girl. We don't do strip clubs."

"And what do you think of it now?"

"Actually, it's kinda hot. But that could just be because of all the hot biker boys roaming around in there." I winked at her as I said that.

"Shame on you, Miss Country."

"Seriously though, Storm has some hot guys. Don't you think?" I was loving this girly chat with her.

She almost spat her coffee at me. "Shit, no!" She shrugged and then added, "Okay, well Nash is pretty fucking hot and has a dirty mouth to go along with it. Don't you ever tell J I said that or I will kill you. Right after he kills Nash. And Griff... Mmm, there's something about him that scares the fuck out of me but at the same time, he does it for me. I don't find any of the other Storm boys hot but remember, I grew up with them so I pretty much just look at them like brothers."

"I met Griff the other night. I know exactly what you're saying about him; he scared the shit out of me too. You wouldn't want to get on his bad side, that's for sure. Nash has hit on me a few times but I can tell that he's the type to do that to anything in a skirt, right?"

"Yeah, Nash doesn't discriminate. He's all about the ladies. Told me once that he's got no interest in ever settling down which is pretty much the same as Scott. I'm just waiting for the day these guys meet a woman who brings them to their knees. It's going to be fun to watch."

I processed what she'd said about Scott. He'd also told me that he didn't do relationships. "Have they ever been in a relationship?"

"I don't know about Nash before he came to the club but definitely not since. And Scott hasn't had a girlfriend since just after high school."

"How old is Scott?"

"He's thirty-four. Why?"

"Well, I'm just wondering how someone gets to be thirty-four and not had a relationship since high school. And let's face it, a high school fling is hardly a real relationship."

"Scott's been pretty focused on Storm his whole life.

And, he's screwed some real nasty bitches. As in, bitches who tried to trap him by getting pregnant from the one time they slept together. That's happened to him twice now, and then there's been the stalkers who wouldn't take no for an answer. Those club whores who are desperate to become an old lady will stop at nothing to get their claws into one of the Storm boys. So, I think Scott's been burnt by women to tell you the truth."

"Scott's got kids?" I was surprised; even though I thought he'd make a good father, I had gotten the impression he didn't have any.

"No. One of them was pregnant but miscarried; thank God. The other bitch was lying but Scott didn't work that out for a couple of months, so she put him through it for awhile."

We sat in silence for a moment, drinking our coffee. I was thinking about Scott; he'd been screwed over like I had. Sure, it was in a different way but still, he'd been screwed because when someone takes your trust like that and stomps all over it, it marks your soul.

"So, what's the deal with you, Scott and Blade?"

"Oh, God! Where to start? Okay, long story short, my Dad screwed around on my Mum and had a child with another woman. That's Blade. But we only found out a couple of months ago. Dad's been hiding his other family all this time. I've gotten to know Blade and like him. I mean, it's not his fault how he came into this world. But Scott's got it in for him and won't give him the time of day. I just stay out of it and have my own relationship with Blade. You've met him; he's okay, right?"

"Holy crap, your family could have its own soap show. Bloody hell. How did your Mum cope when she found out about your Dad? And yes, Blade seems okay from what I've seen."

"I used to think my mother was a strong woman but I'm not so sure anymore. She's still with Dad. I couldn't tell you why though because we've grown apart since all this went down. She's kind of pulled away from me and Scott. I think it's because we've made it clear we want nothing to do with Dad and that we think she should leave him."

"Women do strange things for their men, don't they? My ex cheated on me with my best friend. I left him straight away; would've cut his balls off if I thought the jail time was worth it. But I know lots of women who have stayed under similar circumstances. I don't get it."

"Exactly. If J ever cheated on me, I wouldn't hesitate to cut his balls off; the jail time would so be worth it."

I loved Madison's passion that was so clear in everything she said and did. So different to me; I was more of a laid back, think about it before I do it kind of woman.

She checked her watch. "Shit! I've got to get to work," she exclaimed and jumped up. "Thanks for the coffee and chat; I love hanging out with you."

I stood up too and followed her to the door. "Thanks

for waking me up. Have a good day at work; I'm going to be here struggling to get through it."

She grabbed me for a hug. "Drink lots of coffee. It'll get you through, and I've got it under good authority that the chick who works here makes shit hot coffee."

I hugged her back. "Thanks, and I'll let you know about next Friday night as soon as I know my roster."

"If Scott won't give you the night off, I'll sort him out for you," she said with another wink.

I had that warm, squishy happy feeling in my stomach as I watched her go and sensed the beginning of a beautiful friendship.

14

J walked into the office and dumped a cat cage with Monty on the desk. I looked up at him with a quizzical look.

"I've had enough of the fucking cat. It's yours now."

I threw my pen down and leaned back in my chair, stretching my back and neck as I did it. Chuckling, I said, "Was wondering how long you'd put up with it for."

He placed his hands on the table and leant forward. "You're a lucky motherfucker in so much as I have a hard on for your sister. If I didn't, that cat would've never made its way into my house. Never again, and I don't even care if Madison closes up shop, I'm not fucking budging on this."

"I hate to tell you this, J, but you are so fucking

whipped where Madison is concerned that even a cat couldn't unwhip you, brother. The day I see you say no to her is a day I don't believe will ever come."

He shook his head and gave me a hard glare. Pointing at me, he said, "Mark my fucking words, if a cat shows up at my house, I'll get unwhipped faster than you can say tight pussy."

I highly doubted this but didn't say anything more. Instead, I stood up and said, "Griff's given us the okay to hire that new manager. Can I leave that with you while I take the cat home?" I checked the time; it was just after six pm so I could make sure Lisa had eaten some dinner too.

"Yeah. How's that kid going? Has her mother cleaned herself up yet?"

"Michelle still hasn't gotten her shit together so I check on Lisa every day. If I was sure foster care would be better than what she's got, I'd report it but I refuse to throw Lisa to the wolves when I can watch over her."

I picked up the cat cage and left; Lisa had been waiting long enough for her cat to come home.

I KNOCKED on the door and waited. It only took her a minute to answer, and when she saw me, her face lit up.

"Monty!"

I handed him to her and said, "Can I come in?"

Lisa was so excited and didn't seem fazed by the

ugly wound on his face. That was good because she was going to have to look after him now. She let me in and I headed towards the kitchen, in search of her mother. She wasn't in there, nor was she in the living room.

"She's asleep," Lisa half whispered when she realised what I was doing.

"How long's she been asleep?"

Lisa hesitated, but then replied, "Since just after I got home from school."

Fuck.

"You had dinner?"

She didn't say anything; just shook her head, no, and then stared at the ground.

I reached out and lifted her chin with my finger. We stood staring at each other for a long moment. That fucking mother of hers had a lot to answer for. Finally, I said, "Come on; let's go get you some dinner. I haven't had any either."

We secured Monty in the house and then headed out to a Chinese restaurant because I knew that Lisa liked Chinese.

We'd ordered, and chatted a bit about school, and were eating when she suddenly stood up and said she had to visit the bathroom. When she returned five minutes later, she seemed a little more highly strung than usual.

I tried to catch her eye. "What's wrong? Are you not feeling well or something?"

"I'm okay. It's nothing," she answered, but it wasn't

convincing.

"Lisa, you *were* okay but now you're not. I can tell something's wrong so spit it out."

She shook her head vigorously. "I'm fine."

Christ, I was not equipped to deal with twelve year old girls. I tried to maintain my calm but when she started crying two minutes later, I was out. Grabbing my phone, I tried to call Madison. No answer. Shit. I tried her again, and then I tried J. Neither were answering. Who the fuck else could help me with this? As I was racking my brain trying to figure out who to call, Lisa started really sobbing.

"Hey, darlin', it can't be that bad." I was pretty fucking sure that wasn't what she wanted to hear, but it was all that came to me.

She didn't say anything; just kept sobbing.

Fuck.

In my desperation, I dialed Harlow's number.

She answered almost straight away. "Scott?"

"Thank Christ. I need your help."

"What's up?"

"I've got a twelve year old girl here who won't stop crying and won't talk to me and tell me what's wrong. Don't suppose you could come here and talk to her. You know, girl to girl type shit."

"Umm, okay. Where are you?"

I gave her the directions and she arrived ten minutes

later. Lisa was still crying and not talking. Her body was wracked with sobs now and I felt completely fucking helpless.

Harlow took one look at her and moved to sit next to her, wrapping her arms around her and patting her hair. "Shhh, shhh," she repeated over and over.

Eventually, Lisa started to calm down, at which point, Harlow looked at me and suggested, "Perhaps you could give us a moment?"

Shit, I was more than fucking happy to do that. "Sure, just text me when you're done," I replied, giving her my number and then left them to it.

I spent the next fifteen minutes outside the restaurant, wondering what the hell was wrong with Lisa. If Michelle had fucked up somehow, she'd be answering to me. When I finally got a text from Harlow to come back, I was apprehensive about what I was going to find. But they were standing waiting for me and appeared to be okay.

"We need to go to the shop," Harlow announced, giving me a strange look that reminded me of the look that Madison used to give me when she was telling Dad something that she didn't want me to question.

"Okay -" I was cut off.

"Good, we'll be back soon," Harlow said, confusing me.

"What -" she cut me off again. Now I was getting irritated.

"Just wait here. We won't be long," she asserted, eyes boring into me. It was like she was trying to send me the message to sit down and shut the fuck up. *What the hell*?

I noted Lisa's apparent discomfort with this situation and decided to let it go for now, but Harlow would be telling me what the fuck was going on; I would make sure of that. "Fine, go. I'll wait here," I grumbled and let them go.

While they were gone, I organised for our food to be bagged up to take home. I paid the bill and had just settled the food in my car when I got a call from Griff. "Scott, need you at the clubhouse now; got some trouble here between Marcus and Blade."

"Fuck. I'll be there soon."

I hung up from him and called Harlow. "You going to be long?" I asked when she answered.

"About five minutes, we're just at the convenience store down the road."

"Did you walk there?"

"Yeah. Why?"

"Shit, Harlow, it's not fucking safe to be out walking at night by yourself." I knew that Stoney was tailing her tonight but shit could have still gone down.

"Bloody hell, we're fine. Don't get your panties in a knot," she said, and had the hide to sound pissed at me.

"Wait there. I'm coming to get you," I muttered, and hung up my phone without waiting for a reply.

A couple of minutes later, I was really fucking

annoyed when I met them half way between the restaurant and the convenience store. "I told you to wait there for me," I almost yelled at her.

"And I told you that we were fine," she said calmly, but she was glaring at me, challenging me to argue back.

I stewed on that for a minute before blowing out a long breath. "Christ, woman, why do you have to argue with nearly everything I say?"

"I don't. I only argue with the things you boss me around about," she stated firmly.

"Seems like you argue with everything, babe."

"Seems like you boss me around a lot."

Fuck. She had her hand around my dick and she didn't even know it. Hell, I hardly knew it, but I could damn well feel it.

"Harlow, we need to get back to the restaurant," Lisa interrupted us.

Harlow shot me that look again; the one that said don't question anything. I raised my eyebrows back at her; I was totally fucking clueless as to what was going on here but I kept my mouth shut.

"Okay, honey," Harlow said to Lisa and they started walking towards the restaurant. I followed them, and when we got there, Harlow indicated for me to wait outside while they went in. Again, I followed her direction. While I waited, I received a text message.

Griff: How far are you?

Me: Ten minutes out.

Griff: Hurry up.

Me: Working on it.

I had started pacing by the time the girls came back outside. Lisa seemed calmer now; Harlow had somehow made that happen. Watching them walk towards me, I took in Lisa's smile as they chatted; the smile I'd hardly ever seen on her face. She caught my eye and directed that smile at me.

Smiling back at her, I asked, "All sorted?"

She nodded but didn't say anything.

Harlow agreed, "Yes, but Lisa's still hungry. What happened to all that food you guys had?"

"They packed it up for me and it's in my car. I've got to head out to sort something out. Are you able to take Lisa back to my house and stay with her until I get home? I shouldn't be too long."

Before Harlow could reply, Lisa asked, "Why am I staying at your house, Scott? I can just go home."

I shook my head. "No, your Mum's not in any state to look after you so you can stay with me tonight." I was worried about her and wanted to keep an eye on her tonight.

Looking at Harlow, I asked, "Can you do it?"

"Yes, it's no problem," she replied.

I gave her my address and house keys. "I owe you," I said, as I took the food out of the car and passed it to her.

"Yeah, you do," she agreed, and winked at me, taking the food out of my hands.

As I drove away, I watched them in my rearview mirror; chatting and laughing together. Something settled in my gut, something I'd never felt before. I wasn't sure what it meant, but I was damn sure I wanted this thing at the clubhouse over as quickly as possible.

15

I entered the room and Blade hit my sight. Motherfucker. He couldn't be trusted. Why the fuck was I the only one who saw that?

"Scott, glad you could make it," Blade greeted me as he stood up; cold eyes glued to mine.

I stopped in front of him, and said, "If I'd had more notice you were coming, I would've been here sooner."

Neither of us moved; distrust and contempt thick in the air.

Griff broke the silence. "Blade's changed his mind; he's not willing to halt his distribution into Black Deed's territory."

I snarled at Blade, "What the fuck is your problem?"

Blade held my glare. "Black Deeds pissed a lot of people off under Nix's control. Those people are more than happy to consider a new supplier. If the business is there, I'll take it."

"You've got no fucking idea what hell you're bringing on yourself and your crew with that kind of decision."

"My crew can hold their own."

"You're fucking delusional. Black Deeds will call in other chapters and favours; you won't know what the fuck hit you." Jesus, he was a dickhead and I was fast losing my cool. I knew he'd been bullshitting Dad when he agreed to pull back.

Griff knew my bullshit tolerance level and stepped in. "Scott's right. Black Deeds' power runs deep. They'll smoke you before you even know it."

Blade's face contorted in anger. "Why don't you let me worry about that and you stay out of it? This has got nothing to do with Storm."

My anger had been walking a tightrope and that rope just fucking snapped. "This has got everything to do with Storm. Bullet's asked us to get you to pull out, and if you don't we're in the fucking middle, and on Bullet's shit list."

"Not my fucking problem," Blade snapped.

My fist was itching to connect with his face, however at that moment, my father joined the fray.

"It is your fucking problem," Dad thundered; anger bubbling out of him, "And I'd appreciate it if you'd factor us into your fucking decision. You don't need those coke dollars to survive, so do us all a favour and back the fuck off."

Blade flinched. It was hardly noticeable but I was

studying him, so I saw it. The hard set of his jaw was back in place straight away but he'd been affected by the way Dad spoke to him.

He glared at Dad. "I'll say it one last time, I'm not giving in to that scum. I can't believe you're worried about him. Storm's positioned well; your club can take him if need be."

Dad stepped forcefully towards Blade, his heavy boot thudding with the impact. "What you don't get, son, is that there are times to invite a war, and times to do every fucking thing you can to avoid it. We don't want a war with Black Deeds. You go ahead with your plan, it'll be inviting problems between you and me."

Again, Blade flinched. Interesting; he hadn't been expecting that.

"I'd say our meeting is done," Blade declared, moving to leave. Tension clung to everything in the room and silence filled the space while we watched him go.

"Fuck!" I muttered, running my fingers through my hair.

"Fuck is about right," Dad agreed, looking at me. His face was a picture of stress; the lines of age etched deeply in his skin, and the worry barely hidden. "We'll just have to wait and see how Bullet takes this news."

"You do know where this is headed, don't you?" I asked him.

"Of course, I fucking do. Any fool can see that," he snapped.

"Good, because we're going to have to be ready to strike Blade's crew when the time comes."

He scowled at me. "Hold on one second. Who said that would be the plan?"

"Well, I'm not fucking taking on Black Deeds. You said it, now's not the time to go to war with them. And certainly not over this for fucks sake."

"Scott's right," Griff interjected.

Dad was quiet for a moment, assessing what had been said. "Well, nothing's settled now and if it comes to it, we'll take a meeting."

I nodded. "Agreed."

"I'll see you tomorrow," Dad said, and then left Griff and I alone.

"This isn't going to end well," Griff murmured as he watched Dad go.

"I hear you, brother. I fucking hear you."

L ooking around the room, I tried to get my bearings. I wasn't in my bed but I hadn't woken up enough to instantly remember where I was. Mornings weren't my best time; I needed coffee to function properly before nine o'clock. I took in the grey feature wall to my left, the black and grey colour scheme, and the Harley Davidson print on the wall, and realised I was in Scott's bedroom. It came back to me; after Lisa had gone to sleep in Scott's spare room, I'd decided to lie down until he got home. He must have come home late because I'd fallen asleep, and now it was morning. The early morning light was filtering through his grey curtains; my watch said six thirty.

The bathroom called so I dragged myself out of bed and went in search of it. Scott's home had surprised me. I'd expected messy and undecorated. In reality, it was clean, homely and had some decoration in the form of bike prints, rugs on the wood floor, and I'd even noticed a plant in the kitchen. His house was a Queenslander; I loved the wood and the wrap around verandahs. He'd obviously spent time and money looking after it too because it was in immaculate condition inside and out.

As I walked down the hallway, I glanced at the photos he'd hung on the wall. There was one of an older couple that I suspected could be his parents; looked like his dad was a biker too. The woman in the photo looked like the kind of woman you wouldn't want to get on the wrong side of; tough, and the way she was holding the man was very territorial and protective. In the next photo, I recognised Nash and J. There were some other men in this photo that I didn't know. I really liked this photo, Scott looked happy in it and I bet if I could zoom in on it, I'd see his crinkled eyes. Moving my gaze along the wall, I came to a photo of a gorgeous blonde standing next to Scott who had his arm around her. And this photo had been taken close so I could definitely make out crinkled eyes.

I lingered over that photo. She was beautiful, and they looked so happy and carefree together. I was overcome with a strong desire to know who she was and what she meant to Scott.

"That's Summer; my cousin," a soft voice breathed into my ear.

I was startled and jumped a little. Scott had come up behind me without me even realising. His body was

142 NINA LEVINE

pressed against my back and his breath tickled my ear and neck when he spoke. My skin tingled and butterflies took over my stomach.

I turned and sucked in my breath at the sight of his naked chest that glistened with drops of water. His hair was also wet. I desperately wanted to trail my eyes down his body to see the rest of him but I maintained eye contact instead. And oh, holy mother of God, his eyes were crinkled as he watched me. The butterflies whooshed out of me and desire took hold.

"She's beautiful," I finally managed to get out; his closeness was affecting my ability to think straight.

He took a step back and I caught a glimpse of the towel he was wearing. Pointing at the photos he said, "That's my parents and those are the boys from my club."

"I guessed that was your parents. They look like they're still happy together." Although Madison had told their story, the photo told a different story and I wanted to hear what Scott had to say about it.

He scoffed at that. "It's funny how the outside world can be deceived into thinking something is a certain way. Appearances can be very fucking misleading," he jabbed his finger at the photo, "My parents aren't happy, and any happiness they did have was a fucking lie."

I took in what he'd said, looked at the photo again, and then back at him. "You're right, things aren't always what they seem."

"In my experience, Harlow, things are never as they fucking seem."

His voice had a hard edge to it, and I wondered at what he'd seen and lived through in his life. "Not always, but sometimes they are exactly as they seem," I murmured, "We've just got to open our eyes a little more and when we do see it, we have to believe it the first time and stop second guessing ourselves."

Scott's eyes widened a little, and he leant an arm against the wall. I couldn't help but stare at his arm muscles as he did this; like I said, I had a weakness for arms, and getting a close up of his bare arms like this could not be wasted. "Fuck," was all he said for a moment. His eyes searched mine, and then he said, "They don't make chicks like you around here."

I had no idea what that meant but the mood felt heavy, and I felt the need to lighten it. "I'm all country, baby," I joked, throwing a wink at him, "Now, where's your bathroom?"

He smiled and his eyes crinkled again. Shaking his head at me, he said, "You're something fucking else, you know that?" Pointing at a door down the hall, he directed, "Toilet and shower in there, towels in the cupboard if you want to take a shower."

"Thanks, I think I will."

I felt his eyes burning into me as I walked away from him. When I reached the bathroom, I turned to see if he was still standing there. He was, and the look of desire written across his face sent heat through my body until all my nerve endings were alive with that same desire. It couldn't be denied any longer; I wanted Scott Cole. Simple as that.

I FOUND Scott on his back verandah after I'd finished my shower. He was leaning against the railing, drinking coffee.

"You want a coffee?" he asked, pushing off the railing.

Smiling, I answered, "You have no idea how much I want a coffee. Yes, please."

He nodded, and went inside. I watched him go; he was dressed in the familiar jeans, black t-shirt and his cut. I'd had no idea that's what they called their vest; my mother had enlightened me. I was so clueless about bikers.

"How long have you been a member of Storm?"

"Grew up in it. My Dad's the President." He held up the sugar with a questioning look, to which I shook my head, no. Putting it back down, he asked, "Milk?"

"Yes please, but not too much. And I like my coffee strong."

A couple of minutes later we were back outside, enjoying our morning coffee and the gorgeous spring morning. It was my favourite time of the year, warm without the brutal heat that a Queensland summer can bring.

"Time for you to spill, babe. What was wrong with Lisa last night?" Scott swiveled to face me.

"Girl stuff." I really didn't want to get into it with him; one, because I was fairly sure once he knew what it was he would rather not know, and two, I didn't want to break Lisa's confidence.

He cocked his head with a confused look. "What girl stuff?"

I sighed. "Okay, just remember you asked for this and you can't let on to Lisa that you know. She got her period for the first time last night. That kind of girl stuff."

"Thank fuck you came then. She wouldn't have told me and her mother could care less."

"So, they live next door to you? Are you close?" This relationship had me stumped.

"We're not close but her mother, Michelle, worked at Indigo for awhile. She's a junkie and caused problems there so we had to fire her. Lisa needed a roof over her head so I rented my house next door to Michelle and I keep an eye on Lisa. She knows to ask for help when she needs it but she rarely asks for anything."

"She strikes me as a tough little cookie; a real fighter."

"She is, but she has no fucking confidence. Michelle ignores her and spends her money on drugs before she ever gives Lisa a dime."

"So that's why you brought her cat in and paid for it." I was connecting the dots here and I was surprised where they were leading; not at all what I would have thought. Maybe Scott was more right than I gave him credit for earlier; things and people aren't always what they seem.

"Yeah, babe, that's why I got the damn cat fixed. Lisa loves that cat."

"I get the impression that underneath that badass biker image there's a gentle giant."

"No, there's just me, Harlow. There's no image; I am what I am. Don't fuck with me because I'll fuck back," he said, roughly, eyes piercing mine.

I leant forward, towards him. "I get that, but from where I'm standing, what I see is that for the people who don't fuck with you, you'd give your life for them. And just for the record, I don't fuck with people. Ever."

He stiffened and his jaw muscles tightened. His breathing that had been deep and even was now ragged, and his eyes reached into my soul. I struggled to keep my own breathing even as the intensity of his gaze sent sparks of electricity through me. When he reached his hand up and ran his thumb over my lips, my heart nearly jumped out of my chest and goosebumps flooded my skin.

Our faces were so close now, and when he spoke, his warm breath touched my lips. "The more I get to know you, the more I want to know you," he rasped.

Pleasure shivered through me; from my neck down to my toes. I bit my lip as I took another step closer to him; our bodies now touching. The outside world was blocked out; all I could see, hear and smell now was Scott.

"Fuck," he muttered, and wrapped a hand around the back of my head so he could pull me to him. His lips smashed down on mine and we kissed. I entwined my arms around his bulky frame, letting my hands run over his hard muscles. Scott moved one hand down to cup my ass, and pulled me closer. I'd never be close enough; his body against mine was sheer heaven.

His kiss was rough, yet tender; his tongue tangled with mine in a gentle caress and then it became wild and dominating. I moved my fingers to run through his hair and he grunted in response, and roughly pulled me even closer. My heart was beating so fast now, and my thoughts were scrambled. This kiss was pulling me under; exposing me and laying me vulnerable to a man from a world completely different to my own. And yet, after refusing to give my heart to anyone for so long, here was a man I wanted to open myself up to.

He broke the kiss, and murmured slowly, "Fuck."

"Why do you keep saying that?"

"Because you're making me feel things I never wanted to feel."

"Is that a bad thing?" I asked softly.

"Not sure yet but what I do know is that I've no right to drag you into my world."

"How long do you think it'll take you to work it out? Because I've gotta tell you, I want you; even if just for that one night." His desire for me was causing me to be bold; to be confident in ways I'd never been before. Throwing myself at a man like this was not my signature move.

"Fuck," he growled, again, and leant down to brush his lips roughly over mine.

Of course, I took the opportunity to turn this into another full blown kiss and quickly wrapped my hands around his neck while my tongue played with his and my teeth softly bit his lips. Eventually he pulled away and shook his head at me. "Again, the more I get to know, the more I fucking want."

I was just about to say something when we were interrupted by Lisa. "Scott, is it okay if I go home now to get ready for school?"

Oh, my heart broke for this child. She was twelve but she lacked the confidence that a young girl needed to start her journey through the minefield that was the teenage years. She was average height but so very skinny, her hair was a dirty blonde that hung limply just below her shoulders and she walked with a slight hunch. I wanted to take her home, feed her and pamper her; really, I just wanted to love her because it was obvious she needed it.

"Sure," he replied, and then looked at me, "Harlow will take you."

Lisa gave Scott a look that said 'I don't need help getting home', but I knew where he was coming from so I said, "Come on, let's get you home." I put my arm around her shoulder and walked with her.

Once we were outside and on our own, I said to her, "How are you feeling today, honey? Do you have any period pain?"

Her cheeks flamed red. "No, I don't have any pain. Will I get pain?" Worry etched her face. Bloody hell, her mother hadn't prepared her for any of this.

"Not necessarily but a lot of girls do get pain. I want you to call me if you get some because I will bring you something to help with it. Do you have a mobile phone?" I added that last bit on because it occurred to me that she might not have one.

"Yes, Scott gave me one."

Of course he did. "Pass it here and I'll put my number in it."

We swapped numbers, and then I said, "Lisa, the changes you're going through are going to suck. Well, for a little while anyway, while you get used to them. If you need someone to talk to, I really want you to call me. Okay?"

She agreed before scurrying off to her house to get ready for her day. I waited until she was safely inside her house and then I turned and walked back to Scott's. As I entered his gate, I noticed a motorcycle pull up across the road. I expected the guy to come across but he just sat on his bike and watched me. Strange. But then, what did I know about bikers and how they operated. Maybe he was waiting for Scott and didn't want to go inside. I obviously had a lot to learn.

arlow waltzed back into my house, her short dress teasing me. Kissing her had unleashed something in me; something I wasn't sure would be better leashed. I fucking wanted her, more than I'd wanted any woman. Actually, I'd never wanted anyone in this way. Hell, I'd now had two kisses and the need for more was overpowering. I could only fucking imagine what a night with her in my bed would be like.

"I've given Lisa my phone number so she can call me if she needs to talk girl stuff. I hope that's okay with you," she said.

"Thank you." Jesus, this woman was something else.

"What for?" Confusion littered her face; she really had no fucking idea what that meant to me.

"Babe, you met the kid last night, you don't know her at all, and yet you've shown her more fucking kindness than her own mother. She's not used to people like you but I bet you've touched her in ways you'll never fucking know. You want to give her your phone number? Go right fucking ahead and if anyone's got something to say about it, they'll be answering to me."

"Okay," she whispered, nodding.

"Good. Now, I've got a meeting to get to. And, I want you to get your mother to give me a call later because I want to organise cakes for my restaurants."

"Why do you want cakes for your restaurants?"

"So people can eat them for dessert."

"Smartass," she muttered, and I grinned at her. "Why suddenly do you want them from my mother?"

"Let's just say that someone we both know showed me the error of my ways by not buying my cakes from your mother." Madison had rung me yesterday and nagged me until I agreed.

"Madison," she stated when the penny dropped.

"Yeah. Madison. Now, will you get your mum to call me?"

"Will do," she promised and gathered up her things so we could leave.

As we walked down the front steps, I saw a Black Deeds member parked across the street. What the fuck was he doing here? I ushered Harlow to her car and saw her off before crossing the road to find out.

"Morning," he greeted me with a lazy grin.

"What the fuck are you doing here?"

"Bullet sent me over for a little recon."

"And why the hell are you doing recon on me?"

"For when this shit with Blade goes south. Bullet's gathering info now so he's ready if the time comes. And can I just say, that's some sweet ass you've got there in that blonde."

Motherfucker.

My fist connected with his jaw before I even fully realised what was happening. The crunch of his bones was the most satisfying fucking sound I'd heard in a long time. "You so much as touch her and you'll regret it," I snarled.

I expected him to take a shot at me but he didn't. Holding his jaw he said, "Smart move, asshole. She obviously means something to you."

Fuck.

"Get the fuck out of here, and don't come back."

"See, that depends on whether you convince Blade to pull out of coke."

I'd heard enough. Turning my back on him, I made my way to my bike. We had a meeting with Bullet tomorrow night, and it was not going to go well.

"I WAS JUST ABOUT to call you," she answered her phone.

I smiled to myself; one, her voice was so goddamn sexy, and two, she sounded breathless and excited to hear from me. Those two things turned me the fuck on.

"Need to speak to your Mum, babe."

"Do you call all women babe?"

Where the fuck had that come from? "No. Why?"

"I'm not used to men I've just met calling me babe straight away. You know, usually we have to be dating for a man to call me babe."

"You want me to take you on a date?" Shit, now where the fuck had *that* come from?

"Not necessarily, I just wanted to know if the babe thing was something special."

"It is."

"Okay," she said softly.

"And babe?"

"Yeah?"

"Lunch, today. I'm taking you on a date. Be ready at twelve thirty."

"Scott, you don't have to take me on a date. That was just an example."

"I don't make a habit out of doing things I don't want to do; especially not with women. So, when I say I'm taking you on a date, it's because I want to take you on a date."

"Okay." *Soft again. Christ, that hit the spot.*

"Now, put your Mum on."

Cheryl came on the phone and I placed my cake order and then hung up and sat back in my chair. My dick was so fucking hard right now and my ability to concentrate was shot. I had a shitload of work to do but I needed a break, to clear my head. Leaving the office, I walked out into the bar area of the clubhouse, adjusting myself as I went.

Griff came through the door just after me. "I think I've figured out who's been hanging around Indigo lately and who might have tried to break the back lock," he said.

I gave him my full attention. "Who?"

"A couple of Bullet's boys."

"Shit. What the fuck are they playing at?"

He shrugged. "Your guess is as good as mine."

"I've got a bad feeling about Bullet at the moment. He sent one of his boys around to my place this morning with subtle threats. I think he's betting on Blade continuing his expansion so he's putting a plan into place to come after us as well as Blade."

Griff considered what I'd said. "Sounds about right. Might pay for us to up security at Indigo, plus I'll check our other businesses to see if they've had any problems."

"Good idea. Let Dad know too."

"Will do," he replied, and went to leave, "I'm out for the rest of the afternoon, but I'll be at Indigo tonight to work on that security upgrade."

"Thanks," I said, still contemplating what we'd just discussed about Bullet. After what had happened with Nix, I thought that Bullet had been committed to fixing the relationship between our two clubs. Seems I was wrong.

18

Excitement was bubbling through me. It was nearly time for Scott to arrive for our lunch date. I'd been so surprised that he wanted to go on a date, and had to go home to get changed and do my makeup and hair. I couldn't go on a date without making sure I looked my best. It was a warm day so I'd chosen a pair of denim shorts and a white sleeveless, scoop neck top that I'd paired with some turquoise cowgirl boots and a bunch of silver and turquoise necklaces. I'd blow dried my hair and left my natural waves rather than straightening it like I usually did. My makeup was simple and fairly natural; I wasn't a fan of over the top makeup.

He arrived just before twelve thirty; I liked a man who ran on time so that put him in my good books. Heck, who was I kidding? Scott was so far into those good books now it wasn't funny.

His eyes sought mine the minute he entered the café, and he hit me with a dazzling smile. My legs almost turned to jelly and my heart rate picked up. "You ready to go or have you got things still to do here?"

"I'm ready. I'll just grab my bag," I replied and quickly went and got my bag from the back office. I figured we were on a time schedule here and I didn't want to miss a minute of it.

My mother was chatting with him by the time I made it back out to the front. I watched their interaction; I'd learnt that my mother's intuition when it came to men was pretty spot on. I'd be hanging out to hear what she thought when I returned from the date.

Scott turned to me when he realised I was back. I caught his gaze dropping to my chest and then back up to my face. The sensations this caused in me were something I could get used to; Scott made me feel all woman.

"I was just thanking Scott for his cake order. It's our largest standing order for businesses," my mother said, giving him one of her smiles that she only reserved for people she liked. Holy shit, this was good news. I couldn't recall a boyfriend of mine that she'd ever really liked. "Enjoy your lunch and don't rush back," she said.

Scott directed me to his car. It was the black Charger he'd driven me home in twice now; I'd decided it was probably a 1970's model. I knew this because my father had a Charger when I was younger and I used to help him when he worked on it. Dad's was a 70's model and very similar to this one. Scott's was in amazing condition.

As he opened my door for me, he leant close to my ear and said, "You look gorgeous, babe. It's a good thing I brought my car; couldn't put you on the back of my bike wearing that."

His words, combined with his breath on my neck and his musky smell shot heat through me and I wobbled a little as I got in his car. I took a deep breath and tried to get myself under control while he walked around to his side. It had been many years since I'd been on a first date and I'd never felt this level of anticipation and excitement before. There was also a small amount of apprehension; I might have wanted to have sex with Scott but I knew deep down that this probably wasn't going to go anywhere and I needed to guard my heart from breaking when it all ended. He'd already told me that he didn't take women home and I knew from Madison that he didn't get close to them so I wasn't going to fool myself into thinking that I would be any different.

"Do you like fish and chips?" he asked as he started the car.

"Not fish, but I love prawns and calamari. Where are we going?" His arms were distracting me as they steered the car and changed gears. And that musk smell of his cologne; it was doing things to me that made it hard to concentrate.

"Thought we'd go down to Wynnum. That okay with you?"

"I love Wynnum. Do you go there much?"

"Not as much as I'd like. But the salt air and water helps me process shit in my mind and I need that right about now."

"You know, you keep surprising me."

Glancing at me briefly with a serious look on his face, he said, "Yeah? Well, you do the same to me."

"Can I ask you something about your club?"

"Harlow, you can ask me anything. Can't guarantee I'll answer it though."

"Did you always want to join Storm or did you just do it because your Dad was the President?"

He was quiet for a moment and I figured this was going to be one of those questions he wouldn't answer but then he replied, "I grew up knowing I'd join. It's in my blood. But when I finished high school there was awhile there where I questioned it. I did well in school because my Mum pushed me. I look back now and wonder if she wanted me to have options other than the club. She even made me apply to university and I got accepted into an engineering course. Dad wanted me in the club though and I couldn't fight what was in me."

"Do you regret that choice?"

This time he was quick to answer. "Never. I love my club; they're my family."

I settled back in my seat, enjoying his openness. "So, how does it all work?"

"How does what work?"

"Well, you work for the club right? Do you just earn money from Indigo?"

"We don't run illegal operations if that's what you're asking. Our money comes from businesses that we own."

"What kinds of businesses?"

He raised his eyebrows as he flicked a quick glance at me. "What? You don't believe me?"

"Actually, I do believe you. I'm just curious, that's all. I don't know anything about bikers so I'm just trying to get my head around how it all works."

"You sound like you don't usually believe people. Where's that come from, babe?" His tone was softer now; I could get used to that tone being directed at me.

"You don't really want to hear all about that."

"Wouldn't have asked if I didn't want to know."

My stomach unleashed more butterflies at his words. He hadn't said anything sweet or sexy, but that one sentence said so much to me about him. In my experience with men, and granted I'd chosen some real assholes, they didn't want to get to know me; they wanted to get inside me. So yeah, Scott was all about the butterflies.

"My last boyfriend, Billy, cheated on me with my best friend. He also stole from me; over five thousand dollars that I'd been saving so that I could quit my job eventually and spend my time working towards getting my art into a gallery. This was after living together for three years. Before him was Matt who I dated for a year before I discovered the bullshit life story he'd given me to hide the fact that he was a no hoping bludger who was sucking me dry of money and happiness. Matt came after Neil who -"

Scott cut me off, his voice harsh, "Stop. I don't want to know anymore about those assholes. You ever tell me where they live, they'll wish they'd never set eyes on you." We were stopped at a red light and he focused his eyes on me. There was pain in those eyes but there was also warmth that attached itself to my heart, and I was pretty sure that in that moment, I was his. His to have however he wanted.

The light changed and the moment was broken, but I'd felt it and I wondered if he had too.

"What kind of art do you make?" he asked, and I was thankful for the change in the conversation. I wasn't sure if he'd done that on purpose but I was fast learning that Scott was very intuitive so I wouldn't have been surprised if it was a calculated move.

"Mixed media art."

"Mixed what?"

"It's art that uses a range of mediums, so I mix paint with ink and collage and pretty much anything I want to put on there. I'll show you some of my pieces; that's probably the best way for you to understand what I mean."

He moved his left arm to rest behind my headrest and looked over at me and smiled. "I'd like that." It wasn't his smile so much that hit me; it was the crinkled eyes.

Oh, holy God; I really was done for.

Scott's phone rang at that moment and a male's voice filled the car. "Scott, you got a minute?"

"Griff, I've got Harlow with me but go ahead."

"I've got some information about Black Deeds and our security issues. You good with that?"

"Yeah, brother, shoot."

"It looks like they've been nosing around some of our suppliers, gathering information about our orders and such. Even offered a bribe to one of them to stop our supply. Roughed him up a bit when he refused. I've offered them some muscle until this is dealt with. The other thing is that they've been spotted at some of our other businesses besides Indigo. No other security breaches though."

Scott looked like he was about to blow a fuse. "Christ!"

"Yeah," Griff agreed.

"Keep digging around, and let's start our own fucking recon on them."

"My thoughts exactly. Talk to you later," he said, and ended the call.

I was quiet while Scott processed what Griff had told him. Having no idea what they were talking about and knowing it was none of my business anyway, I refrained from asking him anything about that conversation. We drove in silence for awhile but it wasn't the kind of silence where I was trying desperately to come up with something to say. No, it was an easy silence and I realised that being with Scott *was* easy. Sure, I felt that excited, nervous buzz a little but that had to do with my attraction to him. Just being with him though, was uncomplicated; he put me at ease with the way he treated me.

Eventually, I broke the silence. "Can I ask you another question?"

He chuckled. "Something tells me you're going to anyway."

"What does your Dad do as the President? Because it seems to me like you're in charge of a lot."

"He's handed a lot of the responsibility over to me; getting me ready to take over as President when he steps down. But he still does a lot."

"When will he step down?"

"Not anytime soon. Could be years but I need to be ready."

"Griff didn't want to tell you that stuff with me listening, did he?"

"No, he didn't."

I took that in. Scott said a lot without actually saying a lot.

A couple of minutes later we pulled up to Wynnum Esplanade and Scott parked his car on the road near the wading pool. We went across to Pelican's Nest and he bought us lunch which we took to the park to eat. It was a beautiful day to be out; it kind of felt naughty to be sitting in the sun by the ocean on a work day.

Scott set us up at a picnic table and then asked me, "Is your art something you still want to pursue?"

"Absolutely, and my best friend is helping me find galleries that might be interested in my work."

He scowled. "Wait, this isn't the bitch that cheated with your boyfriend is it?"

"No, I haven't seen her since I discovered that. This is Cassie, my new friend who I'm pretty sure would never do that to me."

"So, you're working on getting your Mum sorted and in the meantime trying to get your art happening?"

"Yeah. And working at a strip club to pay the bills," I winked at him when I said this.

He scowled again. "Harlow, if any of our customers give you trouble I want you to come to me with it and I'll sort them out."

"You seem worried about that but I'm sure I'll be fine."

"I've seen some of those motherfuckers in action, babe. You bring it to me if there's an issue. No-one else; me," he asserted in a way that made his request clear.

"Okay, Mr. Bossy," I teased him but he wasn't in a mood to be teased.

We were sitting across from each other and he dipped his head so that his face was closer to mine. Determination was clear in his eyes. "I'll always be bossy where your safety is concerned. I'm not mucking

around here; these men aren't all your standard Joe
Blow and you need to take that in. They fuck with you,
it means they fuck with me. And babe, I'm not one to be
fucked with," he warned in that deep, threatening voice
I'd heard him use before. The fact that it made me feel
safe didn't escape me. I kind of liked it; no man had
ever made me feel safe like that before.

Later, when he dropped me back at the café, he
reiterated what he'd already said. "Remember, no
putting up with shit from Indigo customers. I want to
know if there are any problems," he said as he met me
on my side of the car.

I only just stopped myself from rolling my
eyes. "Okay."

He moved close to me, backing me up against his
car, his right hand sliding behind my neck and holding
my head. Then he delivered another strong warning.
"Something tells me you don't plan on involving me,
babe, so let me make myself clear. I'm not a man who
likes finding shit out later; especially if something
happened that I could have stopped. There *will* be
problems between you and me if you don't do as I've
said. Understand?"

Shit. Who could argue with that? "I understand," I
agreed.

"Good," he murmured, eyes on my lips, "Now, I
don't do this dating thing so I'm not sure, but I reckon
I'm supposed to get a kiss out of it." His left hand had
made its way to my face and he was holding my cheek.

Smiling, I bantered, "That would only be if you were dating a woman who didn't have a three date policy."

"What the fuck's a three date policy?"

"You take me on three dates before you get a kiss."

His eyes twinkled. "Babe, you're deluding yourself. We've already kissed and you've already made it clear you want me to fuck you. I'd say your three date policy is null and fucking void."

"Well, have you made your mind up about having sex with me yet?"

Smirking, he asked, "Are you trying to bribe me with a kiss for sex, Harlow?"

"Would it work? Because if it would, I'd break my three date policy right here and now."

Leaning even closer to me, he promised, "Fucking you was always on my agenda. First I'm going to fuck you with my tongue, and then I'm going to fill your pretty pussy with my cock. So I'd say it's time for you to give up that sweet mouth."

His dirty mouth sent jolts through me; who would have known that I'd love dirty words so much. I pulled his mouth to mine and kissed him with a passion I'd never known. He devoured me with his mouth, his tongue and his potent desire for me. My body came alive under his touch, and my mind was overrun with lust and thoughts for how I wanted him to possess me. I craved more than this kiss and would make damn sure he fulfilled those promises he'd just made.

Ending the kiss and pulling away from me appeared to be hard for him. "Fuck, baby, that mouth of yours should be fucking illegal."

I smiled. The same could be said about him, but I wasn't telling him that; not yet, anyway. I wasn't handing my heart over to a man that easily anymore.

19

Thoughts of Harlow consumed me for the rest of the fucking afternoon. Christ. This was why I didn't do anything more than one night stands with women. It was distracting me from the business at hand. I couldn't fucking think straight and that was a problem. A problem I didn't have time for at the moment. And yet, every time I thought of her, it warmed my fucking cold heart and drove my dick wild. *Shit. I was fucked.*

I spent the afternoon going over the current Black Deeds problems with Griff, J and Dad. Griff had sent Nash and Stoney to do some of the recon we'd discussed. Bullet's club was involved in drugs and porn. We needed to get a better idea on those operations and this type of thing was Nash's specialty. If there was something to be found out, Nash was the man.

At seven o'clock Mum turned up. She was here for

Dad but I took her aside while Dad was still talking with Griff. "How are you?" I jerked my chin at Dad, "He treating you alright?"

She sighed. "You and Madison need to back off him. He's changing. For the better." She emphasised that last sentence.

"Men like that don't fucking change and you of all women should know that. You've seen enough shit go down in the club, seen enough men who beat their women and cheat on them to know they don't fucking change. When are you going to open your eyes?" I remembered the conversation with Harlow from this morning; she just needed to open her eyes and see what was in front of her.

Flinty eyes hit mine. "Your father has given you everything, Scott, and you need to remember that."

"The way I look at it, he's given me nothing but lies," I fumed.

She flinched at that. "Well you need to look at it a different way."

I shook my head. "Not going to happen," I said, and then added, "Any respect I had is gone, simple as that."

"Kind of makes it hard to work together."

"No, Mum, it doesn't. He's my President, that's it. I get the shit done that needs doing, just like I always have. Any relationship outside of that doesn't exist."

Her voice lowered into a hard, angry tone. "You can be a cold hearted bastard sometimes, Scott. Perhaps it's time for you to learn how to forgive."

She was upset and making a move to leave but I had one more thing to say, "Call me cold hearted, call me whatever you want. I make no fucking apologies for the way I live my life. I do however expect shit from those I love and when it's not delivered or when my trust is broken like that, I will never, I repeat never, fucking forgive or forget. Are we clear?"

Her eyes widened. Then a look of resignation came over her and she walked away.

Fuck. I hadn't meant to be so forceful with her, but the way she was carrying on, like we could all just forgive and play happy fucking families, was not on and it had pissed me off.

I watched her go to Dad. She said something to him and he landed a filthy glare on me before taking her outside. Griff caught this too and whistled once they'd left. "You think you guys will ever sort that out?" he asked as we locked the office.

"No."

"Figured as much."

I checked my watch. "Fuck, Griff, I've gotta go. I want to check on Lisa before I head over to Indigo."

He raised his eyebrows. "Didn't think you were needed there tonight?"

"Not a word, Griff. Not a fucking word."

He held his hands up in mock surrender; huge grin fucking plastered on his face. Griff hardly ever smiled. And whatever he was thinking was probably right. I was screwed.

I FINALLY ARRIVED at Indigo just after nine that night. The place was packed. Scanning the crowd and the bar area, I caught sight of Harlow, and desire slammed into me.

She saw me and her face lit up. I nodded and kept going; I had to get out of there because watching the assholes ogle her was sending my blood pressure through the fucking roof. I ended up in the office, alone with my thoughts. What the fuck was I doing with Harlow? I was looking at breaking two of my rules with her now; never chase a woman, and never fuck an employee. Shit just got messy when you did either of those two things. Problem was though, my dick was committed to making this happen; there was no backing out now.

I looked up as Nash wandered into the office and settled himself in the couch. "Saw you come in, and then saw you dismiss Harlow and come out here. Thought you were into her? Cause I've gotta say, if you're not gonna have a crack at that, I'm into it."

"Leave her the fuck alone, Nash," I snarled, fighting not to jump the desk and deck the motherfucker.

"Yeah, I figured but just had to check." The asshole was fucking grinning at me.

I threw the pen down that I was holding and ran my hands through my hair. "Christ, I've never had a hard on for a woman like I do for her. You ever had that?"

Something crossed his face; a darkness I'd never seen there before but it was gone as fast as it came. "Had it once, brother. Never again."

I nodded slowly. "I hear you."

Then he shocked me by leaning forward in his seat and saying, "Might be right for you though. Never seen a chick get to you like this one."

There was a knock at the door; it was Harlow.

Nash stood up to leave. "Speak of the devil," he muttered, grinning at her as he left.

"What's wrong?" I asked her.

"Amy said to let you know that we need some change for the till. Fives and tens," she replied, not sounding happy.

"What's wrong with you?"

"Nothing."

I'd made my way to her by now. "Don't bullshit me, Harlow."

She tensed and took a moment before saying, "Whatever this is between us, if you're not into it anymore, that's cool with me." She may have said those words but the way she was looking at me told me that it was anything but cool with her.

"Where the fuck did that come from?"

Another pause. "You gave off a vibe when you came in so I figured you'd thought about it and changed your mind."

I reached around and closed the door behind her. Then I backed her up against the door and leaning into her, I rested my arm on the door above her head. "First thing you need to know about me, Harlow, is that I don't tend to change my mind too often. Second thing you need to know is that when I tell a woman I'm going to fuck her, she can be damn sure that I'm going to fuck her. And the third thing you need to know is that I don't like to waste time," I growled that last sentence and grabbed her hip to pull her closer to me before continuing, "Believe me babe, when I say that I'm going to be tasting your pussy soon."

Those eyes of hers widened and just as she went to say something, we were interrupted by Velvet. "Scott," she knocked loudly on the door, "We've got some trouble out front. Nash said to come and get you."

"Shit," I muttered, taking one last look at Harlow before pushing off the wall. "We good?" I asked her.

"Yeah," she said softly and I left her to go and sort this shit out. It couldn't have been worse fucking timing.

Nash was with three guys in the main club area just near the bar. He looked like he was about to take one of them on. "What have we got here, Nash?" I asked, joining them.

His eyes were feral. "Bullet's sent these assholes around," he seethed.

I looked at the three of them. None were wearing their colours and I didn't recognise any of them. "You guys new to Black Deeds?" I asked them.

The biggest one piped up, "No, motherfucker, been around for years, just with a different chapter."

Fuck.

"You in town for long?"

"That depends on how long it takes for Bullet to sort out this little problem he has with your brother."

"My step-fucking-brother, who I have nothing to do with. Perhaps you could remind Bullet of that little fact."

"Bullet doesn't give a shit either way. He just wants this cleaned up, and he doesn't give a fuck how that's achieved. You read me?"

"I fucking read you, dickhead," I snarled before landing a punch on his jaw. I hit him so hard that he stumbled backwards into a table and fell on his ass.

"Nice work, brother," Nash said, and joined the brawl with a punch to one of the other guy's heads.

I didn't waste any time and started in on the third asshole. He was ready though and put up a good fight. Fists and blood were flying, and the sounds of bones crunching were fucking music to my ears.

The guy I was fighting went down for the count so I looked over at Nash to see how he was going. He had everything under control; Nash had some muscle behind him and I'd never seen him lose a fight. However, the first guy I'd decked was back on his feet and heading straight for Nash so I helped out with the guy Nash was going a round with. Approaching the guy from behind, I pushed him hard on his back so he'd lose his balance and when he did, I swung my arm and punched him in the side of his face and shoved him to the ground. On his way down, his face crashed hard into the side of a table and that seemed to knock him out totally.

As I was finishing the guy off, I yelled at Nash, "Behind you, brother!"

He quickly ducked and turned around with an agility that most wouldn't believe he had in him based on his size. I swung my full attention back to the asshole on the ground and bent over and smashed my fist into his face a couple of times. When he finally stopped struggling against me and his body sagged completely, I stood up straight. Nash had just knocked his guy out and was standing over him, watching me. His eyes lit up and he bounced a little on his feet. "Yeah, brother. That was some fun, huh?"

I chuckled. "Yeah, a laugh a fuckin' minute."

I surveyed the club; we'd caused a scene and customers were standing around watching us. Amy and Harlow were standing behind the bar and I saw Harlow say something to Amy but Amy was rooted to the ground with a stunned look on her face and didn't appear to take in whatever Harlow had said to her. Harlow shocked me by wolf whistling to get everyone's attention. It worked, and when she had it, she yelled out, "Half price drinks for the next ten minutes. Come and get it, people."

There was a mad rush to the bar and Harlow's obvious ploy had worked; most customers weren't focused on us anymore. One of the bouncers from outside had come in and he, Nash and I started moving these dickheads outside.

Ten minutes later we had all three of them lying on the ground in the alley next to Indigo. I pulled out my phone and rang Dad. "You need to call Bullet and tell him I've got some of his fuckers passed out in the alley next to the club," I said when he answered.

"What the fuck?"

"Yeah, what the fuck. Three of Black Deed's out of state members rolled in tonight threatening Storm. Nash and I cleaned them up. You tell Bullet we want that meeting brought forward to tomorrow morning. I'm not waiting any longer for this shit."

I hung up without waiting to hear what he said.

"Bullet's got no clue what he's done here," Nash said, voicing what I was already thinking.

"No fuckin' clue," I agreed as we walked back inside.

"Harlow knew what she was doing in there. Pretty fucking impressed with her," he said.

"Yeah."

"What, you got nothing else to say about her?"

"I'm just processing the shit that's gone down lately. Bullet's coming for us and his guy saw me with Harlow this morning. Then we've got those two guys who were watching her the other night. She's been put right in the fuckin' middle of a shit storm."

He didn't say anything else; just nodded in agreement. When we entered the club, everything was

back to normal. One of our bouncers threw us each a
wet towel and I used it to clean the blood off me before
making my way over to Harlow.

"I hope what I did was okay with the half price
drinks," she leant across the bar and breathed into my
ear so that I could hear her over the music.

"More than okay. Thanks for that. You girls
right here?"

"Yeah, we're all good."

"Nash and I have some things to take care of but
we're just out back if you need us."

"Okay," she said as she laid that sexy smile on me.

Before she could pull away from me, I gripped her
hand that she was leaning on. It startled her and I noted
that her breathing picked up. She looked at me
expectantly. "That sexy smile will get you fucked
sooner rather than later, babe."

Her eyes danced with delight. "Oh, I'm counting on
it, big boy."

"Fuck," I growled, "Tonight. You're mine."

Still with the dancing eyes, she leant closer and let
her lips brush softly over mine before saying, "Yes,
tonight I'm yours."

I let go of her hand and we both pulled away but
maintained eye contact. I was transfixed; the world
whirled around me but I was oblivious to it. This
woman had captured my complete attention and I was
helpless to stop it.

Harlow broke eye contact first when a customer

called her away. I stood watching her for another minute or so and then left to go in search of Nash.

I found him with Griff in the office. "How long you been here?" I asked Griff.

"About five minutes. Seems I'm a bit late to the party."

I looked at Nash. "You catch him up?"

"Yeah," he replied.

"Did you find out anything about Black Deed's operations today, Nash?" Griff asked.

"Well it looks like their porn business is going down the drain but I'm still looking into it."

"You keep on that tomorrow while Griff, Dad and I meet with Bullet. The sooner we get that info the better."

The burning anger that I had in me towards Bullet was like a slow uncoiling snake, and God fucking help them when I was ready to strike.

I ripped the red Indigo dress off and stuffed it in my bag. My underwear followed shortly after and then I stepped in the shower. It was nearly three am and I was wide awake. I was at Scott's house after he drove us home when my shift was over. He'd received a call that he had to take so I decided a shower was a good idea while I waited.

The anticipation of sex with Scott had kept me on edge all freaking night and as I soaped myself up I couldn't help but feel turned on while I thought about him. It had been awhile for me and I could hardly wait. In fact, as I finished soaping myself I seriously contemplated marching out there and demanding he end his call.

I poured some shampoo into my palm and then lathered it in my hair. As I turned around to wash it out, I caught sight of Scott leaning against the bathroom door. He was watching me, lust clear in his eyes. I stopped what I was doing momentarily but then decided to just let him watch me while I finished what I was doing. I tilted my head back and reached both arms up to run my fingers through my hair while I rinsed the shampoo out. When I had it all out, I locked eyes with him again for a moment before reaching for the conditioner.

The air was charged with a sexual energy between us. When Scott lifted his t-shirt over his head and then started undoing his belt, I almost couldn't handle the sensations flooding my body. I ran the conditioner through my hair, never breaking eye contact with him. Once he had his belt undone, he popped the button on his jeans and then undid his zip before taking his jeans off. He did all of this with a slow and steady movement that was driving me wild.

He kicked his jeans aside and I lowered my gaze to admire the perfection that was Scott Cole. I ran my eyes over his sinful six pack and his arm muscles that just begged me to touch them. His chest was covered with tattoos, as were his arms. I'd never really been into ink before but Scott's ink got me wetter than I already was.

I moved to rinse the conditioner out of my hair but Scott stopped me. "Don't. I'll do it," he said in that commanding voice that I was slowly growing to love.

I stopped what I was doing and watched him come towards me. When he stepped into the shower and his skin hit mine, I shuddered as jolts of electricity fired

through me. He took charge and rinsed the conditioner
out; his hands gentle rather than rough. Scott doing
gentle just about killed me; God, I needed him
right now.

After he rinsed my hair clean, he angled the shower
head away from us. I wasn't sure why he did this but I
didn't care. Turning to him, I reached my hand up to
grab his hair and pull his face down to mine. A growl
came from deep in his chest and his hand snaked around
me and pulled me to him. His erection hit my stomach
and my pussy tingled with excitement which only
intensified when the hand he had on my ass reached
between my legs and a finger hit my slit. He dipped his
finger in and then out, and ran it from one end of my
pussy to the other. I was so wet for him and moaned
with pleasure. We watched each other while he did this,
our lips centimeters apart but not touching yet.

"I love how wet you are for me, babe," he
murmured while he continued to tease me with his slow
and deliberate hand movements.

I used my hand that was still gripping his hair to pull
his face to mine and I gently bit his lip before laying my
lips on his and slowly kissing him. This kiss threatened
to swallow me; our lips and tongues melded together
and the in and out movement of his tongue almost
matched the in and out movement of his finger at my
pussy. His hard cock jerked against my stomach and I
reached my free hand down and slowly grasped it and
began to move up and down his shaft. As I began to

increase my speed and pressure, he groaned and kissed me harder and deeper until he abruptly pulled away and twisted me so that I was facing the wall. He grabbed my hands and placed them against the wall on either side of me and tilted me so that I was leaning against the wall with my ass slightly out. His hands both grasped my ass, one cheek in each hand. He massaged me and then slowly trailed his hands up my back until they reached my neck. Moving my hair to the side he leant forward and kissed my neck, sucking and gently biting as he went. One hand moved around to cup my breast and he pinched my nipple between his fingers.

I was so lost to him, my body alive from his touch, that I didn't realise he'd knelt behind me until his tongue licked my ass and he nudged my legs apart with his hands.

"Wider, babe," he directed me and I parted my legs wider for him. They were so far apart now that I had to rely on the wall to hold me up. Scott grunted his appreciation and ran both hands over my ass.

"Look down,babe," he bossed me and it turned me on even more than I already was, if that was possible.

I did as he said and watched as he sat on the shower floor and positioned himself under me so that the back of his head was almost against the wall with his mouth in line with my pussy. *Oh, dear Lord. He really was going to kill me.* He ran his hands up my legs and then took my pussy in his mouth. His tongue dipped into me while his thumb massaged my clit. I watched for awhile before the pleasure became too much and I dropped my head against the wall as it overtook me. Between Scott sucking, licking, rubbing and gently biting me, I was close to one of the most intense orgasms I'd ever had. When it hit, my limbs almost gave way and Scott quickly moved from what he was doing to hold me up. I screamed in pleasure and let it take over; allowing him to take my weight and keep me from falling. Eventually, I crumbled into his lap, straddling him, and rested my head on his shoulder.

We sat like that for a couple of minutes before he nudged my head. "Babe, you okay?' he asked in a husky voice.

I lifted my head and looked him in the eyes. "I'm more than okay."

He grinned. "You ready for the next round? Because, I've gotta tell you, my dick is so ready to be in you."

I didn't respond; just kissed him. Madly, passionately and like my life depended on it. Lips, tongues and teeth were colliding in this kiss that set my nerve endings on fire. I pushed myself closer to him. The need to be as close to him as I could was so intense that it was all I could process at the moment. We were skin to skin and I felt like I was right where I was meant to be; Scott felt like my destiny in that moment. The way our bodies moved in unison felt like they'd been made for each other.

He broke the kiss and eyed me wildly. "Fuck. Now, babe. I need you right fucking now."

I nodded. He didn't have to tell me twice; I was completely on the same page. He gripped my hips and moved me so he could enter me. Just as he was about to, he stopped mid thrust and moved me away. "Shit, we need a fucking condom," he muttered.

"Shit," I agreed. Bloody hell, I couldn't believe we'd almost done that.

He smacked me on the ass. "I've got one in my bedroom."

I moved off his lap and we stood up. Stepping out of the shower, I reached for the towel but he put his hand on my arm and stopped me, shaking his head. He turned off the water and then placed his hand on my back and guided me to his bedroom. We dripped water as we went but he didn't seem concerned about it.

As we entered the bedroom, he pointed at the bed, indicating for me to lie down. I'd never had sex with such a dominating man and I decided then and there that I loved being dominated. As I lay on his bed, he stood next to it and watched me while reaching into the top drawer of his bedside table to find a condom. Once he found it, he used his teeth to rip the packet and then he rolled it onto his cock. Good Lord, even the way he did that was a turn on. He held his cock with one hand while rolling the condom on with his other hand and once it was on he reached under and massaged his balls for a moment while his other hand ran up and down his cock a couple of times.

"You still wet, babe? Or do you need me to take care of that again?"

"You have no idea how wet I am for you right now."

He was still sliding his hand up and down his cock; there was no way I wasn't wet but he cocked his head to the side and said, "I need you to show me. Dip your finger in your pussy and touch yourself. Then I want to lick your fingers."

Oh. My. God. Scott had the dirtiest mouth I'd ever had the good fortune of listening to. Without moving my eyes from his, I slipped a finger into my pussy, and then slowly pleasured myself for a minute. Then I pulled it out and rolled onto my side so I was closer to the edge of the bed where he was standing. I reached my hand out so that he could bend down and take my finger in his mouth. He took it all the way in and licked it with his tongue before sliding it back out. We didn't lose eye contact once while this all happened.

"Told you I was wet for you," I purred.

He'd been going pretty slowly all night, but his patience snapped at my words and he moved quickly onto the bed. In one swift movement, he had me on my stomach and he was kneeling on top of me. He pulled my hips up off the bed until I was on my hands and knees. Leaning over me, he whispered in my ear, "You ready for my cock now, sweetheart?"

I didn't answer him, just nodded. He moved back

and positioned himself behind me. Holding onto my hips his cock hit my entrance but he didn't enter me completely straight away. He teased me instead, circling himself over my pussy. It was maddening and I pushed back, hoping to take his cock deep inside.

"Greedy. I fuckin' love greedy," he grunted, and thrust hard and fast inside me. Finally.

His cock filled me and I was in a state of bliss as he thrust in and out, gaining speed as he went. His hands remained on my hips in a firm grasp as he brought me to another orgasm. I squeezed my eyes shut and white lights flashed as I came and screamed his name.

"Fuck babe, I'm gonna come hard. Your pussy is so fuckin' sweet," he grit out just before he lost himself in an orgasm.

I was spent. Waiting until he was finished, I barely held myself up. As soon as I knew he was done, I collapsed onto the bed and lay sprawled on my stomach. He followed closely behind and lay next to me, his hand lazily reaching out and wrapping around my waist. I tried desperately to keep my eyes open but eventually gave in and closed them. My last thought was that my one night with Scott Cole had been so worth it.

21

SCOTT

I checked the time again. It was eight am and Harlow was still asleep. I'd been up for an hour now and was showered and ready for the day. For the past five minutes I'd been standing here watching her sleep, remembering how good it felt to fuck her. She'd gotten under my skin; no other woman had ever made me feel the things I was feeling. I had no idea where we'd go next but what I did know was that I had to get back inside her. Soon.

I was concerned that she might be needed at work this morning so I reluctantly sat on the side of the bed and gently woke her up. It took a couple of minutes but she eventually rolled onto her back and opened her eyes.

"Morning," I smiled at her. Fuck, she was beautiful. My eyes roamed over her body while she woke up some more. A fuckin' glorious sight to start the day with.

"Hi," she said, hesitantly.

I wasn't sure what the hesitation was all about but chose to ignore it for now. "You sleep well?"

"Yes, thanks," she replied in a quiet voice.

Fuck, it was like the Harlow who'd screamed my name last night was gone and had been replaced with someone who wasn't familiar with my cock. I was about to find out what the fuck was going on when my phone rang. I pulled it out of my pocket to see who it was. Shit, it was Griff.

"Sorry, I need to take this," I apologised, holding up my phone.

She nodded and I left the room to talk to Griff. "What's up, Griff?" This had better be important because it was dragging me away from the sweetest pussy I'd ever had in my life.

"The meeting with Bullet is in an hour. I just got word."

"At Gerry's?"

"Yeah, brother. I'll see you there," he said, and disconnected the call.

I walked back down the hall and into my bedroom. Harlow was no longer in my bed. Figuring she was in the bathroom, I headed into the kitchen and put the kettle on to make her a coffee. She joined me about five minutes later, dressed in shorts that barely covered her ass and the tightest fuckin' tank top I'd ever seen. I was instantly hard.

"Fuck, babe. You're killing me here," I said as I handed her a coffee.

"Why?" she asked as she reached up and pulled her hair into a ponytail. I wasn't interested in her hair as much as her tits that jiggled with her arm movements.

"Seriously? You come out here wearing that and you don't know what it does to a man?" And that right fucking there was what turned me on the most about her. If I had the time, I'd rip those shorts off and show her just what the fuck she was doing to me.

"I'll take that as a compliment," she said as she winked at me. Then she took a sip of coffee and asked me, "Can you drop me off at the café?"

That wink almost tipped me over the edge but I managed to keep my shit together. "Yeah. What time do you need to be there?"

"As soon as you can. I want to help Mum with the morning rush."

I picked my keys up off the bench. "Let's go," I said as I shrugged my cut over my shoulders.

She followed me out to the garage and I led her to my car. As I opened her door for her, I followed her gaze to my bike. She stared at it for a moment and then turned to me. "Can we take your bike instead?"

I shook my head. "Not gonna happen while you're wearing what you're wearing. You cover up some skin and we'll discuss it again," I said as I indicated for her to get in the car.

She looked down at what she had on and then back at me with a confused look. "What's wrong with what I'm wearing?"

"We come off the bike, how do you think you'll hold up wearing that?"

It only took her a moment but she got it. Nodding she agreed, "Okay, I get it." She ducked her head and sat in the car but placed a hand on the door to stop me closing it and looked up at me. "But will you take me for a ride one day?"

I stared down at her; listening to her words and hearing that hesitation again. With one arm resting on the top of the car door, I leant into the car and invaded her space. "Just to be crystal fuckin' clear, you'll be on the back of my bike, for any kind of ride you want. You get me?"

She sucked in a breath and her face flushed. *Fuck.* "Time to rock and roll babe, before I pull you back out of the fuckin' car and let you wrap that mouth around my cock," I said as I closed her door. Christ, I needed to get her as far away from me as possible. My concentration was shot to shit and I really needed it to be clear today.

THE FIRST THING I noticed when we pulled up outside the café was the bike parked across the road. The second thing I noticed was that it wasn't a Storm member. And the third thing I noticed was that the motherfucker was leaning against it grinning at me.

I checked my anger and got Harlow safely inside.

Stoney had pulled up down the road; thank fuck I'd called him this morning and arranged for him to keep an eye on Harlow.

"What time are you working till?" I asked her.

Cheryl was behind the counter and piped up. "I only need her for a couple of hours. Should be finished by eleven."

"I'm not leaving you by yourself, Mum," Harlow scowled at her mother.

"Rubbish. You're running yourself ragged working two jobs so I'm sending you home at eleven for some sleep."

Before Harlow could argue anymore, I interjected, "I'll pick you up at eleven and take you home so you can get some rest."

Cheryl sent me a thankful smile and mouthed a thank you to me. I nodded at her and then curled my arm around Harlow's waist and pulled her close so our faces were close. "If you need me, you call me. For anything. Okay?" I didn't want to alarm her by sharing my concerns for her safety with her but I needed her to know she could call me.

"Okay, but I don't think I'll be needing you," she replied.

I roughly pulled her even closer and brushed my lips across hers. "Just make sure you call me if something comes up," I said, gruffly. Christ, would she ever stop arguing with me? Even as I was thinking this I knew that the day she stopped challenging me would be the day I lost interest in her and I fuckin' prayed that she never changed her ways.

I EXITED the café and called Stoney as I walked to my car. "Harlow's here until about eleven, at which point I'll be back to get her. You stay on her till then, and Stoney, guard her like your fuckin' life depends on it. Am I clear?"

"Yeah."

"Good. Also, that bike parked across from the café belongs to one of Bullet's guys. Keep your eye out for trouble from him. And, call me with any problems." I disconnected the call and shoved my phone back into my pocket.

Without giving Bullet's guy my attention, I got in my car and took off to Gerry's for the meeting. Shit was about to go down and I was ready for whatever Bullet threw our way. Storm wasn't a club that you fucked with and Bullet had done just that.

I BARRELED into the back room of Gerry's Café, ready to go to war if fucking necessary. Bullet had succeeded in pissing me off by crossing the line when he sent his boy to my house the other day and again this morning by sending him to the café. He'd jumped the gun and now I'd shove that gun in his face if necessary.

Gerry's Café was where we did most of our meetings and transactions. Gerry had been a member of Storm until his death a few years ago in a deal that had gone south. The motherfuckers had shot him. He'd died too fucking young at fifty and had left behind a family. We made sure his family was looked after and in return his wife let us use the back room when needed. I'd also taken care of the crew that had shot him; they no longer bothered anyone.

Dad and Griff had already arrived, as had Bullet and two of his men. I scowled at them; Bullet didn't look surprised.

Standing, he said, "I see that Spider found you this morning."

I exploded. "Yeah, he fucking did. This shit between you and Blade had nothing to do with us but you've changed that. And there's a world of fucking hurt that comes with that. You want to fuck with my family and with my boys, well have at it, motherfucker, because it'll be the last time you ever try."

"Heard you got a nice piece on the side there," Bullet sneered.

Blood roared to my head and my muscles flexed, ready to lash out. "Like I told Spider, you fucking touch her, I'll kill you."

Bullet stepped into my space, his nostrils flaring and his eyes blazing. "Careful what you threaten there,

Scott. Empty threats still get the same response from me as real ones."

"That wasn't an empty threat, Bullet. You should know by now that I don't fuck around."

A moment passed as we glared at each other. The room was silent; waiting. With one last search of my face, Bullet responded, "I'll give you forty eight hours to get Blade to see some sense but after that, all bets are off." He moved back, away from me.

"The way I'm feeling it, you've signaled that all bets are already off."

Dad agreed with me, "I'd agree with Scott. I think you've made yourself perfectly fucking clear, Bullet." The anger was rolling off him too. Bullet was fucked now; he just didn't know it.

Bullet signaled to his men to leave. "I'll be in touch," he rumbled, and then they were gone.

Fucking hell," Griff muttered. He was pacing the room now; his standard response when shit went down.

"They're watching Harlow's café now," I said to Griff.

"Who the fuck is Harlow?" Dad demanded to know.

"She's a fucking innocent bystander in all of this. And she's a good person who doesn't deserve to be dragged into it."

Griff cut in. "Scott, you need to lock her down. Bullet will come after her now."

"Yeah, I know."

"You've got Stoney watching her at the moment?"

I nodded. "I'll head over there now and take her to the clubhouse."

"We'll meet this afternoon and start working on a plan to take Bullet down," Dad said.

We wrapped things up and then I drove over to the café. This was going to be tricky. Harlow had no clue as to the shit I dealt with; getting her to realise the severity of this situation was going to take some work.

SPIDER WAS STILL outside the café but I ignored him. There were no customers inside and Harlow and Cheryl were nowhere in sight. I rang the bell on the front counter and waited. When Harlow appeared, I muttered, "You really need to put a bell on the door. Anyone could have robbed you by now."

"Well hello to you too," she came back with. "Why'd you put your cranky pants on?"

She had a way of slowing me down when I was angry. I knew I had a bad temper and most of the time I couldn't control it, but with Harlow it was different. She'd say something like she just did, and it would surprise the shit out of me and make me stop and think.

"There's some shit going on that I need to talk to you about. You able to leave now?"

"It's only ten o'clock, Scott. I'm supposed to be here to help Mum for another hour."

"Yeah, I know, babe. I wouldn't ask you if it wasn't important."

She thought about it for a moment and then said, "Okay, let me go and see if she'll be alright without me."

She went out the back and I waited patiently until she returned with her bag. "Mum's okay on her own so let's go."

Thank Christ for that.

22

I put my bag down on the kitchen table and then began opening windows to let some fresh air in the house. It was a warm September day and the house was stuffy. I was a little nervous about what Scott wanted to talk to me about. After last night, I didn't know where we stood. He'd made it clear that he wasn't looking for anything other than one night and from everything that Madison had told me about him, I'd believed that it would only ever be one night. But he'd surprised me this morning, especially when he'd promised me a ride on his bike. And I'd understood his meaning perfectly when he said I could have any kind of ride I wanted. So to say that I was a little confused by it all was an understatement.

I finished opening windows and came back into the kitchen where Scott was leaning against the kitchen bench, arms and legs crossed, a determined look on his face.

"What were you thinking last night when Nash and I cleaned up those three guys at the club?"

Okaay, didn't see that question coming.

"That I'd hate to really piss you off."

He chuckled and it was good to see the serious look disappear for a moment. I liked it better when he let his guard down. I wanted those crinkled eyes again. They didn't make an appearance often enough as far as I was concerned.

"So it didn't turn you off me?"

"Where is this coming from Scott? No, it didn't turn me off you. I think that the fact I spent the night with you proves that."

The serious look was back on his face and his eyes bore into mine. "I want you. I want you in my bed, on the back of my bike and in my life. But my life is a hard one and completely different to anything you've ever known. What you saw last night is just the tip of the iceberg and I need to know that you can handle that shit."

The mood in the room burned with an intensity that I was fast associating with Scott. His words stunned me and I was speechless for a moment. My brain raced to process what he'd said because it was not even in the ballpark of what I'd ever expected to hear from him. If you'd told me that Scott would tell me he wanted me in his life, I would have laughed at you.

Everything I knew about Scott jostled for attention; his temper, his honesty, his compassion, his loyalty to those he loved, his fierceness, his bossiness, his protective streak, and I knew without hesitation that I wanted him too. He wasn't perfect, and I had no idea where we'd end up but I wanted to take a chance on something that could be beautiful.

I walked over to where he was and took his face in my hands. "I can handle that shit."

He groaned and his mouth smashed down onto mine in a rough, passionate kiss. His hands pulled my hips into his and I felt his erection. I ran my hands through his hair and inched my body as close to his as I could get. Being with Scott was thrilling and I knew that I could handle any of his shit so long as I had him in my life.

I could have stayed like that forever but Scott broke the kiss and pulled away from me. "I'm counting on it, babe, because we're about to hit a shit storm."

"Talk to me. Tell me what's going on."

He blew out a breath before continuing. "My club has some enemies and one of them saw me with you the other day and then again this morning. They haven't come out and made threats against you but I take their actions alone as a threat. I can keep you safe while we deal with this but I can only do that if you drop out of sight for awhile."

"What does all of that really mean?" Drop out of

sight for a while? I wasn't sure where he was heading with this.

"Babe, it means exactly what you think it means. The guy that's made this threat is a nasty motherfucker and I take everything he says and does seriously. Deadly fucking seriously. What I want you to do is stay at the clubhouse until this is dealt with. You good with that?"

"How long do you think I'd be staying at the clubhouse? Because I can't leave my mum to deal with the café by herself."

"I don't know how long this will take. Could be a couple of days or more."

"Then I'm not okay with staying there. I can't just put my life on hold like that."

"I'm not asking you to put your life on hold; just to drop out of sight for a little while so we can keep you safe. I can organise help for your mum at the café."

"No, Scott, she needs someone who knows the café."

He was getting agitated. I could tell by the vein popping in his neck and the way he was rubbing the back of his neck. It was too bad though; I wasn't bailing on my mum when she needed me.

"I know I said I wanted you, and I fuckin' do, but Christ, you'll be the fuckin' death of me, woman."

I stood my ground. "I've laid down and let too many men walk all over me in the past, Scott. I won't do it again. Maybe you need to be the one to decide whether you can handle *that* shit."

He didn't even think about it; he just growled, "Babe, I can handle that shit and more."

Butterflies took over my stomach and his growly voice set my nerves alight with excitement. I smiled at him. "Good, because there's a lot of baggage for you to sort through."

As we stood watching each other, we were interrupted by a knock at my front door. I moved to go and answer it but Scott put his hand on my arm and shook his head. "Wait here, I'll get it."

I didn't say anything but on the inside I was rolling my eyes. Seriously, if someone was coming to get me, why would they knock on the door? I moved out of the way and let him go and be my caveman. A moment later I heard Cassie's voice and laughed out loud. "Thanks for saving my ass, Scott. You've got to watch out for Cassie cause you never know when she's going to pull her ninja moves out and try and hurt you," I yelled out.

He came back into the room with a scowl on his face. "I can tell that you're taking this seriously."

I took pity on him because he really did look annoyed and I knew that he was just trying to look out for me. "Sorry. Just trying to lighten the mood," I apologised, and then ignoring the surprised look on his face, I waved my hand between the two of them and said, "Scott, meet my best friend, Cassie. Cassie, meet my caveman, Scott."

Her eyes widened. I hadn't had a chance to fill her in on anything that had happened the last few days. She was a good friend though; she didn't quiz me on it in front of Scott. That would be girl catch up time conversation. Instead she asked, "What have I missed here? What's Scott saving you from?"

"Just some biker stuff that's going on. Now tell me, to what do I owe the pleasure of your visit?" I was trying to give her the hint that I wanted to talk to her about this in private.

She picked up on my message and smiled at me in that knowing friend way. "I haven't heard from you in a little while so I thought I'd drop in and see how you are. Your mum told me you had the day off."

Scott broke into our conversation. "Ladies, as much as I'd love to shoot the shit with you, I've got business to get back to. Harlow, this conversation is to be continued but for the moment, I've got one of my boys watching you so you'll be safe."

"What do you mean, you've got one of your boys watching me?" I was so not used to the way Scott did things and I was struggling to get my head around it.

"I mean, if you look outside, you'll see one of my men on his bike guarding you. Anyone tries to get to you, they've got to go through him first and he's not an easy fucker to get past. You go out anywhere, he'll be following you."

"Damn. I need me a caveman like you," Cassie said, and I didn't fail to notice the breathlessness in her voice. Oh, good Lord, she was sucked in to the Scott Cole bossy charm.

I shooed him. "Okay, fine. Got you. I've got my own personal bodyguard. Thank you. Now, go and leave us girls to talk about you."

He shook his head in a 'what the fuck am I getting myself into' kind of way. But then he pulled me in for a kiss and smacked my ass before he began walking out of the room. "Get some sleep, babe. I've got plans for you tonight." And then he was gone and my skin was tingling with excitement.

After we heard the front door close, Cassie turned to me and shrieked, "Fucking hell! Spill the beans, girl."

We spent the next hour over coffee and cake while I caught her up on what was happening between me and Scott.

"So, you're together now?" she asked.

I shrugged. "He was pretty clear that he wants me in his life, but you know what? For once in my life, I'm just going with the flow and not forcing something. I don't know him that well yet so I want to take my time working him out."

"And are you worried about this threat that's been made? It sounds scary; like do you really want to get involved with someone who brings that type of stuff into your life?"

"I know I should probably be running the other way but I've seen Scott in action and I believe that when he says he can keep me safe, he'll keep me safe. And, I've lived my whole life picking guys that I thought were the better option. I've always gone for the men who I thought were the good guy. And, they all screwed me over one way or the other. Scott might be a biker and be involved with trouble but he's shown me so many other sides to himself that are worth something more than anything those other assholes gave me."

"Yeah, you can't always judge someone by their outwards appearance can you?"

I smiled mischievously. "Well, Scott's pretty hot to look at... I'd say you'd be right to judge him as the guy most likely to give you an amazing orgasm."

"Oh my God. I need to know more!"

I got up from the table. "We need more coffee for this."

Cassie was grinning at me like a mad woman; talking men was one of our favourite things to do. I laughed at her and sent a message of thanks out to the universe for blessing me with the best friend a girl could want.

"**S**cott." I turned at the sound of my father's voice. We'd just finished meeting with the club to plan our next move. Nash had shared his findings with us. He'd discovered that Black Deeds owed close to half a million on their porn production company and that they were struggling to pay it off. It seemed that their drug business was the only way they were currently able to meet their monthly debt bill. That was why they were so hell bent on keeping Blade out of it. Our goal now was to hit them where it hurt; we just had to come up with a plan to do that.

I stopped and waited for him to catch up to me. "What's up?" I asked him when he got closer.

"I want you to come with me to see Blade. We need to bring him up to speed."

My immediate reaction was to decline but I thought about it for a minute. I came to the conclusion that I'd prefer to be involved in this meeting to make sure that Dad didn't agree to something that wasn't in Storm's best interest. "You want to go now?"

Dad's face flickered surprise for a moment. "Yeah. He's at his warehouse; I'll meet you there."

I agreed and he left. As I was walking to my bike, Harlow called me. "You okay?" I answered it.

"Yes, but I just wanted to let you know that I got a call from Lisa. She's upset because some of the girls have been bullying her today. I'm going to go and see her at school and make sure she's alright. Is that okay with you?"

"Babe, already told you, you want to help Lisa, you go right ahead. Anyone with a problem about that answers to me."

She was quiet for a moment. "Okay," she replied, softly.

"Let me know if there's anything you need from me, otherwise I'll see you tonight. I'll be over at about nine o'clock to pick you up."

"Okay," she breathed into the phone and it made my dick jerk.

"And babe, cover up because I'm putting you on the back of my bike tonight," I promised before ending the call. Christ, just the thought of her on my bike, pussy tucked in close and arms around me, made me hard.

I'd just put my phone back in my pocket when a text sounded. I pulled it out to check who it was from and just about came on the spot.

Harlow: I'll cover up for the ride on your bike but when I ride your cock there'll be nothing separating my pussy from you.

Me: Fuck, woman. That dirty mouth of yours is gonna get you in trouble one day.

Harlow: Promises, promises…

Shit. I jammed my phone back in my pocket before she continued to tease me and my dick. How the hell had an asshole like me been lucky enough to find a woman who was so pure and yet so dirty at the same time?

"So, you're telling me that you do want to start a war with Black Deeds now." Blade concluded from everything we'd just told him. His hard eyes were glued to mine.

"We need to hit them before they hit us," Dad said.

Blade moved his gaze away from me to Dad and then leant back in his chair. We were sitting in his office. It was an impressive looking office with all the latest technology. Actually, Blade's whole setup was quite flash; it didn't fit with the image I had of him as a seedy, drug dealing scumbag. His warehouse was large, very clean, sleek and looked to be well organised from what I'd seen walking through it to the office. I'd also caught a quick glimpse of his security room and he appeared to have high end stuff. He also had a lot of men working for him; another surprise to me.

After a long pause where it seemed that he was weighing something up in his mind, he leant forward again and said, "We've been tracking Black Deeds for a long time. Some of them are the lowest fucking scum on Earth as far as I'm concerned, and trust me, I've dealt with some scum. After a thorough analysis of their operation we decided to target their porn business. We've almost crippled them there. They rely on their drug trade to pay their porn debt. Without their drug business they can't service the debt. We're working on taking their drug business away from them."

Fuck. I'd seriously underestimated Blade. "The coke business isn't what you're after at all, is it?"

"No." Those hard eyes hit mine again, and I had to wonder what lay behind them; what made him tick.

"Care to enlighten us as to what is?" Dad asked what I was thinking.

Blade paused again. "Bullet and some other members will be eliminated and Black Deeds will be rebuilt by a new president."

"You do realise they have other chapters they'll call in, don't you? It won't just be this chapter you have to deal with."

"I'm not a man who doesn't finish what he started. I'm also a very patient man. This plan has been in place for two years and the research on it was conducted over the prior year. Those other chapters won't be a problem; I can assure you of that."

My father was looking at Blade like he hardly knew him. "You've been working on this for three years and I never knew about it?"

Blade's face contorted in anger, and he shoved his chair back and stood. "What do you know about me, Marcus? Tell me what the fuck you actually know about me," he thundered.

I settled in to hear this. Looked like Blade and I had something in common after all; a burning contempt for our father.

"I thought I knew that you ran a gang that was involved in robberies, prostitution and drugs."

"Turns out you were wrong," Blade snapped.

"Would have been nice for my son to tell me the truth."

"What the fuck do you know about being truthful?" The anger swirling around Blade was palpable; I was starting to think he had more anger in him than I had in me.

Dad looked like he was about to explode with his own anger. Fuck, we were just one big happy fucking family. I stepped forward and broke through their tense standoff. "Blade, what's the reason? What have you got against Black Deeds?"

The pain that ran across his face was clear and appeared to run deep. "Three years ago, Bullet and three of his club members murdered my girlfriend. Ashley and I had been together for five years and were planning to get married. This particular night she was out with friends celebrating one of their birthdays. She tried to call me to come pick her up but I missed her call. From what the police worked out, her drink was spiked at some point and they took her after that. They gang raped her and slit her throat. Same as what they did to Madison's friend."

"Christ," I muttered, the horror of it hitting me and dissipating some of my hostility towards him.

He nodded. "Since investigating them, I've discovered there are more women out there who've died at their hands."

"So why not just kill them and be done with it?" Dad asked.

"The current VP of Black Deeds wants out of porn and drugs. He's watched what you've done with Storm and wants something similar; something that doesn't bring them so much heat. He and I have been working together to make that happen. It would have been easier just to kill them but this way I've gotten to watch Bullet shit himself while he's been losing everything he's worked towards. Easy revenge doesn't give the same sense of satisfaction as this has."

Blade was one cold and ruthless man, that was for sure. The fact that he'd calculated this plan in such detail put him in that category.

"So, where does that leave us and our current problem?" I asked.

"To start with, those guys from the other chapter that came to your club have been taken care of. And if any more turn up, they'll be dealt with also. My men had been watching your club to try and stop Black Deeds from fucking with you but the night they came in, we were dealing with another issue -"

I cut him off. "So your men weren't watching Harlow?"

"No, not in particular. They did report back about her though. Being a new staff member, I had her investigated to make sure she was clean. Incidentally, she is."

"I know that, asshole."

He shrugged. "Can't trust anyone these days, Scott. Black Deeds have been trying to screw you by messing with your stock distribution for your businesses but I've taken care of that too. Now, as for Bullet. I was scheduled to take him out in two weeks but in light of his threats against Harlow, I'll see if we can move that up."

"I want in on that, Blade," I demanded.

"We'll coordinate with you and any of your men that want in."

"I also want this to happen soon." I needed this to happen quickly; there was no way I was leaving Harlow in danger while we waited around for Blade to get his plan working.

His hard glare penetrated mine. "I've said what will

happen; you just need to sit tight and have some patience. Harlow will be kept safe."

I scowled at him. "Yeah, she damn well will be because I'll be making sure of it. You hurry this the fuck up or we'll take shit into our own hands.

24

I knocked on her door and then stepped back, waiting for her to answer. It was just after ten pm and I was at least an hour late after being held up at Indigo. The new manager was still getting his bearings; I hoped to Christ he didn't take long working it all out because I'd had enough of being there every day.

Harlow opened the door wearing jeans and a t-shirt. I ran my eyes over her body and appreciated everything she had on offer.

"My eyes are up here," she joked as she reached out and lifted my chin so that I was looking at her face.

I took a step forward, curled my arm around her waist, pulled her close, and growled, "I was getting there, babe. You've just got too damn much for a man to look at all at once."

Her breathing picked up, and she murmured, "Take

your time. I like your eyes on me." She wrapped her arms around me and threaded her fingers through my hair before her lips found mine in a searing kiss.

Kissing Harlow was unlike kissing any other woman. She made me feel alive in a way that no one else had. Most women were in it for them; what they could get out of me. They were always looking for more from me; more that I didn't want to give them. Harlow wasn't looking for a damn thing. And she didn't take my shit. I could respect a woman who respected herself enough to stand her ground. As much as it fucking pained me sometimes.

She ended the kiss and raised a querying eyebrow at what was in my hand. "What's that?"

I gave it to her. "Picked it up for you this afternoon. Put it on."

She smiled; her excitement obvious. "I love it!" she exclaimed as she put it on. "I've always wanted a leather jacket."

"Yeah, well whenever you're on the bike, I want you in this."

Her smile could have lit up the whole fucking world. "You're making me all squishy," she said, her eyes twinkling.

"Babe, I have no idea what that means but if it's gonna get me laid tonight, I'm fuckin' glad that I'm making you all squishy."

"As much as I love listening to your dirty mouth, I'd

rather be enjoying it in another way so can we move this along?"

Christ. She didn't have to ask me twice.

"Get your stuff. I need to get you naked and under me."

I had plans for her tonight and she was going to love my dirty mouth by the end of it.

"THAT WAS SO MUCH FUN!" Harlow waltzed into my house, her cheeks flushed with excitement. It was the first time she'd ever been on a bike and it was pretty evident that she loved it as much as I did.

I chuckled and followed her inside, dumping my keys on the bench in the kitchen. She put her bag down too and turned to me. "When can we go on a long ride?"

My hand curved around her neck and I pulled her to me. "You pick a day and I'll be there," I murmured as I brought my mouth down onto hers. She embraced me and her lips parted, letting my tongue in to tangle with hers. I deepened the kiss and moved my hand down her back to rest on her ass. My other hand reached under her t-shirt and searched for her tits. When I found them, I pushed her bra aside so her breast spilled out into my hand. Harlow had a good handful; just what I loved. I twisted her nipple between my fingers and the gasp she let out hit me in the dick. My kiss became rough; demanding.

Harlow pulled away from me; her lips swollen from our kiss. I didn't let go of her though, and continued to massage her breast. She maintained eye contact as she pulled her shirt over her head and tossed it on the floor. I moved both hands to the back of her bra and undid it, freeing her breasts. As I dropped her bra on the floor, she undid the button on my jeans and lowered the zip; her hand grazing my hard cock.

I stood still, my eyes trained on hers. "I want your mouth on my cock," I demanded.

Without taking her eyes off me, she reached in and wrapped her hand around me, and started to slowly move her hand up and down my length. As she got to the end she gently ran her thumb over the tip, spreading my pre-cum over my dick. I didn't stop watching her even though I wanted to look down and take in the glorious fucking sight of her hand on my cock.

"You'll have my mouth soon," she promised, "but first, I want to play with you with my hands."

Fuck me.

She kept moving her hand up and down my dick as she said, "Take your jeans off."

I wasn't used to a woman taking the lead during sex but this was fucking sexy as hell so I went with it. Once they were off, she gripped my cock hard and used it to gently pull me closer to her.

"Christ, babe. Careful there," I muttered, but I had to admit that that turned me on too.

A wicked glint flickered in her eyes as she leant her

mouth almost on mine and breathed out, "I'm going to make you come so hard you'll be seeing stars."

Fuck. I almost came right fucking then.

The slow movement of her hand on my dick mixed with the sight of her tits moving as she did this, and her breath on my lips had sensations ricocheting through my body, making me feel things I'd never felt during sex. And fuck, we'd only just started.

"You ready?" she asked.

"Babe, I was ready for your hands and lips on my cock the minute I laid eyes on you," I growled.

She added her other hand to her maddening tease of my dick. One hand moved down my length, and then the other. She gently twisted my dick each time, and it nearly blew my damn mind. I dropped my head back and closed my eyes; those stars she'd mentioned were floating behind my eyes. I was getting close to blowing my load. Just when I thought I couldn't wait any longer, she stopped. My eyes snapped open and I found her watching me.

"Do you want my mouth on you now?" she asked.

"Fuck babe, you even gotta ask that?"

Her lips curled into a sexy smile. "Just making sure," she said with a wink, and before I could blink she was down on her knees and my dick had her lips wrapped around it.

Fuck. Nothing fucking compared.

Her warm breath felt amazing as she took me deep into her mouth. Her sucking was gentle to begin with but she began to pick up the pace, and at the same time she started to massage my balls with one hand. When she grasped the back of my leg with her other hand and then moved that hand slowly up to my ass, I jerked forward and the tip of my cock hit the back of her throat.

"Fuck babe, I'm gonna come," I rasped, gripping her hair harder.

And fuck me if she didn't keep sucking and licking. I rolled my head back, shut my eyes and let the orgasm take over me completely. She'd been fucking right; I saw stars. As she kept sucking me and massaging my balls and ass, I felt it build until I thrust my hips forward and came hard in her mouth. She didn't stop sucking and swallowed everything I gave her.

When my body stopped jerking, she slowly slid my dick out of her mouth, looked up at me and then licked the tip clean. I reached my arms under hers and pulled her up. When our faces were at the same level, I muttered, "Now that's what I call a blow job."

She smiled. "You saw stars?"

I smirked. "Babe, I saw the whole fucking universe."

She lazily kissed me and the taste of me on her had my dick jerking to attention again.

"I want your pussy," I murmured as I backed her up against the table. Thank fuck I kept this table clear because I was about to lay her out on it and sink myself into her.

She moaned as I kissed her again and then I tilted her head back with my hand and trailed kisses down her neck. When I lightly bit her, she dug her fingernails into my arms. I pulled back a little to look at her. "You like that, baby?"

Her eyes were full of raw lust and she simply nodded. Then she surprised me by grasping my head with both her hands and directing my lips back to her neck. I didn't need to be told twice and I kissed and sucked her neck while my hands massaged her tits. I kept this up until her hands met mine and she dragged them down to her jeans button. Having a woman take the lead turned me the fuck on and I did what she wanted. A moment later her jeans were off and then I hooked my fingers on her panties and ripped them down too.

Now that she was naked, I stepped back to admire her beauty. Christ, she was stunning. My eyes roamed over her breasts, stomach, pussy, legs and then back to her pussy. She was bare there and I loved it. I reached a hand out and dipped one finger in. She was so wet and I slid right in so I inserted a second finger and watched her eyes glaze over with pleasure.

"Feel good, baby?" I asked, as I ran my thumb over her clit while I finger fucked her.

She moaned and nodded. "Yes," she finally got out, her breathing ragged.

I kept up a good pace and had to use my other hand to hold her up as she began to lose herself in an orgasm.

Christ, watching Harlow come was a spectacular sight. She started to moan and mutter my name; it sounded so fucking good on her lips. A man could get used to this.

Right before she came, I dipped my mouth to her breast and sucked on her nipple, adding some teeth every now and then. She seemed to like that as her hands came up and held my head down in place. Her body shuddered and she screamed out my name as she came. When her body went limp, I wrapped both arms around her to hold her up.

We stood still for awhile; holding onto each other. I was turned on and couldn't wait to get inside her, but I was also feeling something else. My heart felt full; happiness snaked through me. This was a new sensation for me and I wasn't sure what the fuck it meant but it felt so damn good. It was the kind of sensation that made you want to never break away from whatever was causing it. I gripped Harlow harder; in this moment, I never wanted to let her go.

She moved and I loosened my hold on her. Her eyes found mine and she smiled. "A man who knows what he's doing; I like that about you."

I grinned. "I always aim to please."

"Well, I'll keep you around for awhile longer then." Those eyes were dancing and teasing me with their wickedness.

"You fuckin' better," I growled, and brushed my lips against hers. "Babe, my dick needs to feel your pussy."

She kissed me hard and reached down to stroke my

dick. My eyes squeezed shut for a moment; her touch felt so fucking good. Breaking the kiss, she moaned, "Now baby. I'm ready."

In one swift movement, I put my arms around her ass and lifted her so that she was sitting on the table. I kissed her and then said, "Just getting a condom."

I grabbed my jeans off the floor and searched in my wallet for it before coming back to her. She watched me intently as I undid the wrapper and slid the condom on. "Lay back, baby," I said, moving right up close to the table, "and rest your legs on my shoulders."

Her eyes widened before a look of excitement took over, and she did what I said. I ran my hands over her legs while I enjoyed the view of her laid out on the table. "Time to fly, sweetheart," I said, gruffly, before lifting her ass off the table and gripping her waist as I lined her pussy up with my cock. Holding her waist, I pulled her towards me and thrust in.

"Fuck! Scott... feels so good, don't stop," she screamed and started panting as I kept thrusting in and out slowly. Her arms flung out so that she could grip the sides of the table while I fucked her.

I continued my slow thrusting and felt my orgasm build. This position was one of my favourites but with Harlow it was out of this fucking world. Watching her pant, and watching her tits move as I moved her body in time with mine was an amazing fucking sight. My orgasm was so close but I was holding off for her. "You close?" I grunted.

Unable to speak, she nodded. I needed to hurry this up or else I was going to blow my load without getting her off first. "Touch yourself, babe."

Surprise flickered on her face and she was hesitant. Fuck me, I fucking loved that about her. Touching herself in front of a man must be something she hadn't done much, and I was more than fucking happy to change that. "Baby, touch your pussy. It'll get you off faster. I'm ready to come but I want you to go first."

She didn't hesitate this time. My eyes greedily tracked her hand down to her pussy and my dick almost exploded with pleasure when she started rubbing her clit. It was obviously good for her too because her hips began to jerk and I watched as her eyes fluttered shut. Her pussy clenched and that was fucking it for me. I came and a moment later she screamed out as she orgasmed too.

After a moment in which I still held her ass up off the table and let us finish, she opened her eyes and shot me the sexiest look she'd ever given me. "You weren't joking when you said it was time to fly, were you?"

I chuckled and lowered her to the table before pulling out. "No babe, I don't make promises I can't keep."

She sighed; completely sated. "Good, because I've been looking for a man who makes good on his promises."

My heart constricted. For the first time in my life, I wanted to be a man who made promises to a woman.

25

I stepped out of the shower and dried myself before wrapping the towel around me. Scott was leaning against the doorframe watching me closely. For once, his eyes weren't on my body but rather they stayed focused on my face. I smiled at him but he was in a serious mood and didn't smile back. Sometimes his intensity freaked me a little; now was one of those moments. We'd just had the best sex of my life and I had felt so close to him; I wondered what was running through his mind after that.

"I want to know more about you than I've ever wanted to know about anyone," he said. It wasn't at all what I'd expected him to say.

"What do you want to know?" I asked.

"Everything," he said, forcefully.

Butterflies whooshed through my stomach. Every woman dreamed of finding a man who wanted to take the time to get to know them. I'd dated a lot of men but never found one who'd ever said anything like that to me. His request was so genuine and straight from the heart. Standing in this bathroom with Scott's full attention on me, I felt like the Queen of the world; he made me feel like that. Scott might be a biker who said and did things that most people wouldn't ever dream of doing, but he was the first man who gave me the confidence to be completely me. He was unapologetic about the way he lived his life and he gave me the same freedom; the freedom to be whoever I was and to live my life on my terms.

I moved closer, reached for his hand, and laced my fingers through his. "I want to know everything about you, too."

He blew out a breath and tightened his fingers around mine. "I've never met a woman who wanted to know me. Sure, they said they wanted to be with me but that didn't mean they actually wanted to know anything about me. But you're different and I knew it from that first time we met."

"What do you mean, you knew I was different? How?" I certainly didn't feel like I was different from anyone else. I'd struggled my whole life to make myself stand out; I always believed I was the boring girl that people overlooked.

"Fuck, Harlow, you don't see it, do you?"

"No," I confessed in a whisper while I held my breath waiting for him to continue.

He let go of my hand and lightly ran a finger through my hair, pushing it off my face. His touch was so gentle; so different to the rough way he liked to touch me during sex. "You stood up to me and challenged me. You still do. No woman has ever done that before. You're a strong woman, and you're kind and giving. Look at the way you're helping your mum. Look at how you took Lisa under your wing after you just met her. I don't know many women who give so selflessly like you do. And yet, there's a softness to you that I haven't worked out yet but I like it. I like it a fucking lot."

"I thought I was going to be the death of you by arguing with you."

"Yeah, babe, you will be. But promise me that you won't ever stop because it'd be the death of you if you did that."

I knew in that moment that I'd just completely fallen for Scott Cole. Any man who totally got that about me would hold me captive, and he now had me for as long as he wanted me.

I gently laid a hand on his bare chest. "I promise."

His hand curled around my waist and he roughly pulled me close so that we were skin to skin. "You've got me under your fuckin' spell and I can't get enough of you," he growled.

The room was charged with electricity as we connected mind, body and soul. The sound of our breathing was the only noise to fill the room while we were silently watching each other.

Scott's phone ringing in his bedroom cut through our moment, and he reluctantly pulled away. "Sorry, I've gotta get that," he muttered as he finally broke eye contact and left the room.

After he left, I let out a long breath and steadied myself against the door. The intensity of that encounter had left me in a state of wanting a whole lot more but at the same time, needing a moment to regroup. Being with Scott was going to involve a whirlwind of emotions; I just hoped I was strong enough to sustain them all.

SCOTT LAY his arm across my pillow and pulled me to him so that my head was on his chest. It was just after two am and we'd been lying in bed talking for awhile now. I was exhausted after not much sleep last night and then a long day again today. Scott didn't seem as wiped as I was though; he was in a talkative mood.

"So, your Dad passed away when you were a teenager?" he asked. He'd been asking me about my family; trying to work it all out in his head.

"Yes, he died of a heart attack. It was so unexpected because he was such a healthy, fit man. Mum was devastated and I don't think she's ever fully gotten over it. She's only been on a handful of dates and doesn't seem interested in finding a man. The café is her life now."

"When did she move to Brisbane?"

"She left Gympie a few years after Dad died. I was eighteen when she left; I think the memories were too much for her there. Brisbane was where she grew up so it was a natural choice for her."

"That must have been hard for you?"

"Yeah, it was. After Dad died, I felt lost. It was just me and Mum then, and so when she left, I felt completely alone. I mean, I had my friends but I've always been a family person so I felt alone without either of them around. Mum bought her café and started working every day. It was her way of trying to forget the pain, I think. But it meant she blocked me out, even though she didn't mean to."

He was quiet for a moment while he processed what I'd said. "So you had no family with you and then the two people you trusted like family did the fucking dirty on you by cheating with each other."

I sucked in a breath. How did he get me so well? Sometimes it felt like he was in my head. "Yes," I answered softly.

"People can be motherfuckers sometimes. Family too. But you know what? Family doesn't always share the same blood. My boys are my family. I'd do anything for them and they'd do the same for me."

"That's what Storm's all about isn't it?"

"Yeah. It's about family. We might argue and annoy the shit outta each other but when it comes down to it, we're there when needed. We know we can count on each other. That's what makes us as strong as we are."

"I like that," I murmured, feeling really sleepy now.

He kissed the top of my head and squeezed me closer to him. "Night, baby."

I fell asleep feeling the happiest I'd felt in a very long time.

"So, you two have been dating for a week now, right?" Madison asked Harlow as I was on my phone, pacing the room while I waited for Blade to come back on the line. We'd been discussing the Black Deed's situation when he'd been called away for a moment. Harlow and I had dropped into Madison and J's house after a bike ride. I'd taken her on a long ride; we'd started out early, just after six this morning and ridden up to Mount Tamborine and then down to the Gold Coast. It was now just after three o'clock and Madison had asked us to stay for an early dinner. Harlow was keen but I just wanted to get her home; having her that close to me on the bike all day had made my dick permanently hard.

I listened to Harlow's response. "Yes, we're taking it slow, seeing where it's heading."

What the fuck?

I moved the phone away from my mouth, and looked Harlow in the eyes. "We're not *seeing* where this is headed, babe. I know where this is headed."

Her eyebrows shot up. "Really? Where is this headed, Scott?"

Always demanding; always challenging. Fuck, I was a lucky bastard.

At that moment, Blade came back on the phone and I didn't have time to answer her. I walked outside to finish the call.

"Everything's in place; we'll be taking out Bullet in two days," Blade said.

"I don't want to wait two more fucking days, Blade. Bullet's breathing down our necks at the moment about you. He's on edge and capable of God-knows-fucking-what."

"I met with him last night to discuss the coke issue. He believes that I'm about to agree to pull out of drugs. That should buy us enough time."

I wasn't convinced but was willing to give him those two days. After that, all bets were off; Storm would take care of the problem.

We finished the call, and I looked up to see J coming through the back door. He'd been at the hardware store when we got here; Madison had him doing some redecorating.

I lifted my chin at him. "You get everything you need?"

He sat in one of their outdoor chairs. "Probably not.

Madison can't make up her mind on colours so I'm at the hardware store every second day picking up a new sample for her."

I sat too, and raked my fingers through my hair. "This shit with Black Deeds should be over in two days. Just got the call from Blade."

"You trust him now?"

"I believe what he's told us about Bullet and what happened with his girlfriend years ago. The pain I saw on his face can't be faked. Not sure about anything else where he's concerned but there's a whole lot more about him that we don't know. Of that I'm sure."

J nodded. "Fair enough. So, what's the plan?"

"Don't know yet, brother. He'll let us know closer to time."

My attention was diverted when Harlow came out and joined us. She came and stood next to my chair and rested her hand on the back of it. I reached my arm around her waist and pulled her onto my lap. "Has Madison decided what we're doing for dinner yet?" I asked.

"She suggested we go out; she's still annoyed that we had to cancel our girl's night out last Friday. She figures that we'll be okay if you and J are with us." She lifted her arm so that it was across the back of my chair and started gently running her fingers up and down my neck.

"She knows that we cancelled that night out for both of yours safety. Jesus, she holds onto stuff," I muttered.

Her fingers on the back of my neck were messing with my concentration.

"Where does she want to go?" J asked, getting up.

Harlow shrugged, her eyes lost in mine, and her attention to J's question waning. "Not sure," she finally answered him.

J chuckled. "I'll leave you two to it," he said, and went inside, leaving us alone.

I tightened my hold on her and brushed my lips against hers. "You're turning me into a fuckin' pussy."

Her face broke out in a smile. "I like that. You're so much easier to control when you're a pussy."

I growled. "You don't want to control me, baby. You like bossy too much; it fuckin' turns you on."

"Scott, since I met you, I've lived in a constant turned on state. It doesn't matter if you're being bossy or being a pussy, I can't get enough of you."

"Fuck, woman. You got any idea what it does to me when you say shit like that?"

She grinned, and whispered in my ear, "I hope it gets you hard so that you'll fuck me as soon as we get back to your place."

Christ, I was fucking done for now. Dirty words coming out of Harlow's mouth almost made me come there and then. I smacked her ass. "Up. We're skipping dinner; I'm taking you home now."

"Thank goodness. I never thought you'd suggest it so I had to give you a prod," she said with a wink.

I shook my head. "Harlow, any time that you want

me to fuck you? Just say the word; you'll never hear no from me."

Twenty minutes later, I had Harlow right where I wanted her; naked and under me. Best fucking way to end a day.

I was dozing on the couch when my phone rang. Sleep wasn't my friend lately in between working two jobs and Scott keeping me up late every night. Grumbling, I reached out to the coffee table to answer it. Checking the caller ID, I noticed it was Lisa calling me. Worry hit my gut; why else would she be calling other than if she had a problem. I'd had to go up to her school last week and help her make a complaint about being bullied; I hoped this wasn't still going on.

"Hi Lisa," I answered, trying to project an upbeat attitude.

"Hi Harlow," she said in her timid voice.

"What's up, honey?"

She started crying and my heart hurt listening to her. "Where are you?" I asked. It wasn't quite three o'clock so I figured she was probably still at school.

She sniffed. "I'm in the toilets at school. Can you

come and get me?" she begged.

"Yes, I'll be there soon. Just wait where you are; I'll find you."

Just under ten minutes later, I pulled up at her school and followed the directions she'd sent in her text as to where she was. When I found the toilets, I entered and called out to her. A door opened and she stepped out; her face was a mess from crying, and her hair was an uneven mess. Someone had cut her hair and screwed it up completely.

I waited for her to say something but she didn't so I went to her and simply took her in my arms and hugged her. She slowly wrapped her arms around me and then squeezed tighter until she was practically clinging to me; her body wracked with sobs.

We held each other for nearly ten minutes while I waited for her crying to subside. Eventually she pulled away from me and I asked, "What happened?"

"They cut my hair and hit me."

"Who did that?" I wanted to throttle whoever did this to Lisa.

"I don't want to talk about it. Can you just take me home?"

I wanted to talk about it; I needed to know the names of these little shits. But I put Lisa's needs first. "Of course I can do that," I said and indicated for us to leave. "Come on, let's go."

She already had her schoolbag with her; she must have been planning her escape. I got her into my car and started driving towards my house. "Do you mind if we just drop by my house first because I think I left windows open. It's sort of on the way to your house."

"Sure," she agreed.

When we arrived at my house, I made Lisa wait in the car while I quickly ducked inside to shut the windows. I figured that Scott would be annoyed if he knew I'd left them open. As I entered the house, I smelt a smell that I'd never smelt there before. It was a putrid, sweat smell and I quickly covered my nose. I kept walking to the kitchen and came to a stop when I saw what was waiting for me there. My heart froze and panic spread throughout my body.

"Well, hello there, sweetheart," the biggest guy said with a smile that scared the shit out of me. His eyes flicked over me and he licked his lips He was sweaty and filthy looking and I prayed to God that he wasn't left alone with me because I wasn't sure I'd survive anything he did to me.

My legs turned to jelly and I threw out a hand to steady myself against the wall.

"Cat got your tongue?" he leered at me and started walking my way.

I tried to back up but another guy came up behind me and grabbed me, roughly shoving me forward towards the scary guy. Hands reached out and gripped my neck, and in one clean movement, he reefed me forward and turned me before planting me on the seat that was waiting for me.

My heart was beating rapidly now and my arms felt tingly from the fear I was experiencing. Why had I decided to come home and close the freaking windows?

"So, you're Scott Cole's woman? Never known him to have a broad."

"We just met," I answered him, desperately hoping that it would make a difference to him that I hadn't known Scott for very long.

His evil laugh sent chills up my spine. "What bad timing for you then, darlin'."

My mind was racing frantically trying to come up with a way to escape but I just couldn't see a way out. There were three of them and one of me. Where the hell was Stoney? Tears pricked my eyes; I was sure I was about to die at the hands of these assholes.

"What do you want from me?" I begged.

"We're actually here to teach Scott a lesson. He's fucked with us and we don't appreciate it. Unlucky for you, especially if you've just met the motherfucker."

Another man entered the room and he was even scarier looking than any of these men. His eyes were void of any emotion and his body was tense; he looked like what I always imagined a cold hearted killer would look like. He threw rope at the scary guy. "Tie her hands and legs. I've got some calls I'm waiting for and after those we'll get the party started." He was standing right next to me now and he ran a finger down my cheek. "Scott's got good taste. I can't wait to hear you scream."

N ash settled into the couch in the office. "So, Blade's going to let us know the plan soon?"

"Tonight, and then tomorrow it'll be done," I said, distracted by the fact that Stoney wasn't answering his phone. I'd been trying to call him for ten minutes with no luck. "Have you heard from Stoney today?"

"No, why?"

"He's watching Harlow but he's not answering his phone."

"You want me to go and check that everything's alright?"

"No, I'll go," I said as I stood up.

I was halfway down the hall when Lisa called me. "Hey darlin', you okay?"

"Scott, I'm outside Harlow's house because she picked me up from school but had to come home to close windows. She's been inside for ages and I saw a man just come out to have a smoke. I don't think he's from your club. Can you come here and see if she's okay?"

Fuck!

"On my way, darlin'. Stay where you are and hide if you can. Do not go inside, Lisa. Okay?"

"Okay," she answered me and we hung up.

"Nash!" I bellowed down the hallway. When he appeared at the door, I yelled, "Black Deeds have Harlow at her house."

"Fuck!" He followed me outside.

There was going to be fucking hell to pay for this.

WE PULLED our bikes up a couple of houses down from Harlow's and ran the rest of the way. There were four bikes parked further down the street; I felt ill thinking about what we were going to find inside. Harlow's car was parked in the driveway and I tapped on the window to get Lisa's attention.

"I want you to run that way," I said, pointing down the street, "Keep going until you hit the shopping centre and wait there. I'll either come get you or I'll send someone."

She nodded fearfully, but did as I said. It would be safer for her there than here.

Nash was already at the front door. He eyed me. "I

sent a message to J to round the boys up. Hopefully they'll be here soon but we're going in regardless, yeah?"

"Yeah." I pulled out my piece and looked at him, "Ready?"

When he nodded, I lifted my foot and with as much force as I could muster, kicked the door in. We entered and were soon greeted by three Black Deeds members. Nash lived for this shit and charged them. They obviously hadn't been expecting either of us to do that and he managed to catch them unprepared. He knocked the first motherfucker out and then took aim at the next one. While he took those two on, I punched the third one hard on the jaw, knocking his face to the side. He stumbled from the impact, and hit the wall. I shoved him to try and get him off balance and then followed as he lurched backwards, punching him again on the other side of his face. He tried to regain his balance but I'd managed to put him off, and he fell to the ground. I hovered over him and punched him repeatedly in the face until he passed out.

Nash was still fighting with the second guy who was giving him a good run for his money. Fighting was in Nash's blood and I'd never seen anyone get the better of him. Whenever I had something that needed to be taken care of with violence, Nash was my man. It was like he zoned out into another state of consciousness, and the punches just kept flying. However, the guy he was fighting was holding his own so I got in there and threw a couple of punches too. After a couple of minutes, I decided to try another tack. I lifted my leg and kicked him fair in the balls. He doubled over and this gave Nash the perfect opportunity to pistol whip him on the head. When the guy finally collapsed face first onto the ground, Nash reefed him up and turned him onto his back. He was semi-conscious and Nash wanted him knocked the fuck out so he kicked him hard in the head. He kicked him a few times and would have kept going except the first guy we knocked down, sat up and took aim, shooting Nash in the arm. The bullet grazed him and slowed him down but didn't bring him to a complete halt; he had too much adrenaline pumping through him for that. Instead, he turned his attention to the guy that shot him, knocked the gun out of his hand and lunged at him; wielding a punch as he went.

"You motherfucking asshole," he roared as he finally knocked him unconscious. Turning to me, he asked, "You want me to put a bullet in these assholes?"

I shook my head. "No, they're out for the count and Blade wants to deal with them himself."

Stopping to listen for sounds in the house, I realised that I could hear a whimpering sound coming from down the hall; from the direction of Harlow's bedroom. Fear mixed with adrenaline and I took off in that direction. I was blinded by desperation; nothing would have stopped me from reaching my destination at that moment. When we hit her bedroom, I was sickened by the sight we found. Harlow was gagged, and laid out naked on her bed, her hands tied to the bed above her head, and her feet tied to the bedposts. She was conscious and her terrified eyes locked onto mine, silently begging me to save her. Bullet was straddling her, holding a knife to her neck.

"Fuck," Nash thundered, and Bullet turned feral eyes on us. In that moment, I fully grasped what a madman he was. I started to move into the room, mentally calculating how the fuck I was going to get Harlow out of this alive.

"Don't take another fucking step, or I'll slash her throat quicker than you can blink," Bullet threatened, pressing the knife harder against her neck. He pressed it hard enough to draw blood, and Harlow whimpered. Her cheeks were damp from her tears and I experienced a pain in my chest that I'd never felt before; like it would fucking explode and my heart would shatter to a million pieces if I didn't get her out of there.

"Let her go, Bullet, and the coke is all yours again," came a deathly calm voice from behind me.

Blade.

Bullet madly jabbed his finger in my direction. "Get him the fuck out of here, and we'll talk."

"Not fucking happening, motherfucker," I roared.

"Scott," Blade urged, "Would be best if you did as he said." As he said this, he jerked his head at one of his men who had also turned up. The communication between Blade and his man was flawless even without words, and the guy grabbed me from behind and pulled me away from the room. Harlow's eyes turned wild and her body began violently jerking as she watched me go. I fought it but the guy had a strong hold on me and another one helped him so between them, I had no hope.

The last I saw of Harlow was her fucking terrified for her life; I just hoped that Blade knew what he was doing. If anything happened to Harlow, I wouldn't hesitate to kill every last fucking man involved.

29

My father.

That's what I was thinking of as I was lying naked and tied to a bed, with a psycho on top of me and a knife to my neck. My life flashed before my eyes and the only good thing I could think of was that I would get to see my father in heaven after this asshole murdered me.

When they dragged Scott away, I felt like my life truly was over. They'd taken Nash at the same time so I was left with Blade. I had no idea how he'd gotten mixed up in all of this. All I knew about Blade was that he was Madison's half brother and seemed okay whenever I'd made him coffee and chatted to him. But whether he had it in him to save my life? I had no clue. And that scared the ever loving shit out of me.

Blade moved into the room, and his presence filled the room. "You need to get the fuck off her, Bullet, if you want me to back off the coke." His voice was commanding and there was a tone there that screamed authority. I made eye contact with him; his eyes were cold but when they hit mine, they softened and I saw the warmth there. The fear and uncertainty swirling in my gut eased in that moment.

Bullet pulled the knife away from my neck and moved off me. Facing Blade, he snarled, "And why the fuck would I believe anything you say?"

Blade shrugged. He was so cold and calm, and I decided that I'd never want to get on his wrong side; I'd be more afraid of him than Bullet, and that was saying something. "Scott's my brother, and she's his woman. I don't need the coke to survive; I think you're aware of that fact. So, if I have to choose between the two, I choose her life."

Bullet thought about it and settled it in his mind. "I'll take that fucking deal but if you break your word, I'll go on a killing rampage like you've never seen before, and you'll be my first port of call. Right after I fuck her and make sure her death is a long and painful one."

I flinched at his threat. Fear sliced through me and I prayed to God that Blade would keep his end of the bargain.

Blade nodded once. "Good. Now, get the fuck out of here," he commanded in that deep, frightening voice he had.

I watched frantically while Bullet left the room.

When he'd finally exited and I could no longer see him, I let go of the control I'd employed throughout the ordeal. I wanted to scream, kick and punch all in one go but I couldn't. Instead, I started shaking and sobbing, and struggled to catch my breath as my breathing became erratic.

Blade moved towards me and pulled a knife out. He cut the ropes that had bound me to the bed and removed the gag from my mouth. Then he took the sheet and covered my body. His movements were all gentle and deliberate. He was safe; I knew it in that instant. He would never hurt me.

He sat on the bed beside me. "You need to know that everything's going to be okay. The threats that Bullet made towards you will never eventuate because he will be taken care of. He won't be walking this earth long enough to carry those threats out. Do you understand?"

Words failed me so I nodded.

"Good." He stood back up and moved to leave the room. He turned at the door and said, "Scott will be in in a minute."

And then he was gone. I took a long deep breath and attempted to get my breathing and shaking under control. Right now, I needed Scott more than I'd ever needed anything.

30

I found her huddled under the sheet, her tear stained face was all that was visible. Thank fuck Blade had covered her up. She slid her eyes to mine and what I saw there nearly fucking killed me.

A moment later, I sat on the bed next to her, and just after that she was in my arms; clinging to me and crying. "He touch you?" I asked; I needed to know, because if he had, there was no way I was letting Blade be the only one to fuck him up.

She shook her head vigorously. "No."

"Thank fuck," I muttered, although it was a small mercy considering everything else he'd put her through.

"Scott, Lisa's outside waiting in the car. You need to go and make sure she's alright."

Fuck. This was why I was falling for Harlow; in a moment where most women would buckle from what they'd just been through, she was more concerned for someone else's safety.

"No, she's safe. I've got someone with her."

"Thank God," she said, the concern washing off her face.

I reached up and gently wiped the tears from her eyes. "I'm so sorry, baby. This is all my fault."

She nodded and then asked, "Remember when I said that I could handle your shit?"

"Yeah."

"Well, if you feel the need to hurt those assholes, and when I say hurt, I mean so that they can never threaten another woman with that, you need to know that I can handle that shit, baby."

Fuck me. Blessed. That's what I was.

"Good to know. Because I'll be making damn sure that they'll never hurt another person. Now sweetheart, we need to get you cleaned up."

She nodded in agreement, and I helped her into the shower. The deep burning hatred I had for Bullet was consuming my thoughts, and I hoped to hell that Blade was making him suffer.

SIX HOURS LATER, Harlow was asleep in my bed. She hadn't wanted to stay at her mum's house that night so I'd brought her to mine. I'd spent all afternoon and night with her; I hadn't called J or Nash to find out what had happened. This was the first time in my life that I'd put Storm second. I never wanted to let Harlow out of my sight ever again. Knowing her, though, that would never happen.

I stood in the doorway and watched her sleep. She'd had trouble getting to sleep so I'd found a sleeping pill of mine to give her that had eventually done the trick. My phone vibrated with a message.

Blade: You want in on this?

Me: Yes, but not tonight. Tomorrow.

Blade: Call me when you're ready.

I watched Harlow for a little while longer and then I went outside to call Dad.

"Scott, thought I would have heard from you by now," he said, not even a hello to greet me.

I ignored him. "You hear from Blade?"

"Yeah, he's got the men he wanted. They were the four at Harlow's house. The VP of Black Deeds stepped up and took over; he's made sure there's no blowback on Storm for this. But those fuckers killed Stoney to get to Harlow."

"Fuck!" In my gut I'd known that; it was the only explanation for everything. Stoney wouldn't have gone down without a fight so they would have had to kill him.

"How's Harlow?"

"She's fine but I didn't call to chat; I just needed to know that everything had been taken care of and it has, so I'll talk to you later."

I disconnected the call without waiting for him to say anything else. My patience for my father was growing less and less every day.

I PULLED the café door open and waited for Harlow to walk in before I followed her. Cheryl was waiting for her, and enveloped her in a hug. They embraced for a long time; her mother gently patting her hair. She'd spent some time with Harlow last night but I imagined her distress as a mother would be unspeakable.

"Thank you, Scott," Cheryl said as they pulled apart.

Fuck, I was the last person she should be thanking; if it wasn't for me, Harlow would never have been put in that situation. I shook my head. "No, it's my fault. Don't thank me."

"No, it's not. Did you tell that man to do what he did? Did you have any control over his actions? No. People do shitty things all the time; they're responsible for their own actions. Not anyone else. So, don't ever blame yourself for this."

Christ, I saw where Harlow got her purity from.

"Thank you," I murmured, still uneasy about it all.

Harlow turned to me, and the gentle look she gave me, softened my hard heart a little. "She's right. This wasn't your fault. Okay?"

We hadn't talked much this morning; both of us still contemplative. So, I had no idea what was going through her mind about all of this. I was giving her some time to process it; tonight we would talk.

I nodded. "Babe, you gonna be alright if I leave now?" I had to be at Blade's within the next hour to take care of Bullet and that was one meeting I didn't want to be late for.

"Yes. You go and do your stuff. I'll be here all day. Can I stay with you again tonight?"

As if she had to ask. "I'll be here to pick you up at five. Yeah?"

"Five is good. I'll see you then," she said, and leant forward to give me a quick kiss.

Five minutes later, I was on my way to take care of Harlow's request to make sure that Bullet couldn't fuck with any other women.

I couldn't deny it - I was a twisted fuck sometimes. The idea of fucking Bullet up made me one of the happiest men on the fucking earth that day. And when I entered the room where Blade had him, I realised that my half brother and I shared more than a father; we shared a darkness inside us that only physical violence could sate.

The room was on the lower level of Blade's warehouse and was a concrete room with clear plastic lining every surface; the roof, walls and floor were all lined with it. And I was sure that once we'd finished here today, that plastic would be replaced with new plastic for the next occupant of this room.

Bullet was laid out naked on a table, his arms and legs restrained in the same fashion that Harlow had been. I noted that Blade was wearing a black outfit of training pants, t-shirt, and runners. He indicated to a table in the corner of the room that had an identical outfit laid out. "Change room is through there," he pointed to the corner where there was a door.

I grabbed the outfit and headed towards the corner. The plastic was cut so that I could get through and I entered a large open shower. I quickly changed and joined Blade again. He had a determined look on his face as he asked me, "You ready?"

"More than fucking ready."

Bullet was shifting his gaze between Blade and I, and I was pleased to see he had that wild look in his eyes that I'd seen in Harlow's yesterday.

Yeah that's right, motherfucker. Your turn now.

I had no idea what Blade had planned here. He obviously used this room for similar operations and had a very well thought out set up in place so I was just following his lead. He picked up a knife and lightly ran it down Bullet's body from his throat to his dick. "You know why they call me Blade?" he asked.

Bullet shook his head, clearly shitting himself.

"It's because a knife is my favourite killing weapon. My first kill was when I was seventeen; I killed a man with my bare hands, finishing him off with a blade twisted into his throat."

I watched him intently, taking this new information in. All clues today were pointing to a cold blooded killer, and I had the thought again that I'd underestimated Blade.

He looked at me while he spoke. "From what I've

heard, Scott's good with his fists, so I'm going to let him go first today." He took his knife and cut the ropes restraining Bullet, and shoved him off the table, towards me. Bullet took the opportunity now that he was unrestrained, to try and get a punch in. He was too slow for me though; I threw a punch so hard that it knocked him to the floor. He landed flat on his stomach; there was a loud cracking noise as his face smashed onto the concrete floor.

He didn't move, and Blade muttered, "Fuck, did you knock him out?"

We watched as he lay still, but were both fucking happy when he moved and tried to get up. I let him take his time getting up; I was enjoying the anticipation. He finally stood and then faced me. I was pretty fucking ecstatic to see his face had been fucked up. That had to hurt. He stumbled towards me; the motherfucker was still trying to get one in. I let him come at me but there was no way he had the upper hand here, and I easily punched him again. He fell down again, and I walked to where he was and kicked him hard in the side. He rolled and grunted but he didn't have it in him to get back up.

Looking at Blade, I suggested, "You hold him up while I punch the shit out of him?"

Blade nodded and then moved to drag him up off the floor. He held him and then invited me to go for it. I didn't need to be asked twice. All the anger I had in me for what he'd done to Harlow came pouring out through my fists as I connected with his body time after time. I loved working with a punching bag but a human punching bag was even better. Eventually he sagged, almost unconscious, and Blade signaled for me to stop. We dragged him back to the table and laid him down.

His head lolled to the side and he groaned in pain.

"Open your eyes, asshole," Blade commanded.

Bullet opened his eyes a slit but then snapped them shut again. Blade picked up his knife and with a quick flick of the wrist, he sliced into Bullet's dick. Bullet's eyes snapped open and he screamed out in pain. *Best fucking sound I'd heard all day.*

"That was for Harlow," Blade said, "And this is for Ashley." He ran the knife slowly down Bullet's body again, before suddenly lifting it up and violently stabbing it into his gut. Then he pulled it out and stabbed again, this time in the chest. His eyes were cold and hard as he continued to stab Bullet. There was blood everywhere. I lost count of how many times he stabbed but it had to be over twenty times. Finally, he stabbed into Bullet's neck and twisted the knife as it went in. He left the knife in there and then sunk to the ground. I had no idea what he was doing until I saw his body was wracked with sobs; his back heaving.

"Leave," he grit out, still not looking at me.

I knew when a man was broken and when they needed to be alone so I left him to it. I exited through the door to the shower where I stripped and dumped my clothes in the rubbish he had set up in there. Then I showered and washed all the blood off me. I was coated

in it. Once I was completely clean of it, I changed back
into my clothes and left through another door that I
guessed would take me back into the warehouse. I was
correct and quickly found the building exit. Once I was
out, I took a moment to catch my breath. That had been
an intense experience; not so much because we'd killed
Bullet, but more because we'd put our differences aside
and come together to do it. Blade had revealed himself
to me today, in more ways than one, and I knew it was
going to take me some time to work through it in
my mind.

LATER THAT NIGHT, I watched Harlow get ready for bed.
I was sitting on the bed, leaning against the headboard.
She was at the end of the bed changing out of her
clothes into my t-shirt that she'd started wearing
sometimes. After her ordeal with Bullet, I wasn't sure
where her head was at with regards to sex. I had no
desire to push her but I wanted to talk to her about it; to
make sure she was okay.

She finished changing and then climbed into bed
next to me. Her eyes found mine and she smiled. "I'm
exhausted. Do you mind if I go to sleep?" she asked.

I slid down the bed so that I was lying next to her,
on my side. "We should talk about Bullet."

"What about him?" she asked. There was tenseness
in her voice that hadn't been there before.

"Sweetheart, he almost raped you. I need to know how that's affecting you."

She took a moment to answer me but then said, "I fucking hate him for it and it's not something that I'll move past straight away. But I'm not going to let him win. He did this to both of us, Scott. Sure, I was the one he physically attacked but he did it to fuck with you and it did. So, we'll work through it together. I won't shut you out so long as you don't shut me out."

"I don't know what the fuck I did to deserve a woman as good as you," I said as I lightly brushed a kiss against her forehead.

"I think we both lucked out," she replied, wrapping herself around my heart a little more.

I grabbed the container with the cake in it and got out of my car. Surveying the building, I took in the Storm logo above the front door. It was a huge logo with wings, a skull and flames coming out of the skull. There was a chain threaded through the image. In my mind the chain symbolised the bonds that held the club together. Family. It was so evident when you sat back and watched the way the club members interacted. I'd now been to two get togethers with the club and I visited the clubhouse nearly every day. And the best thing? They'd welcomed me with open arms.

I pushed through the front doors and made my way to the kitchen. When I got there, I was excited to see that Madison was already there waiting for me.

"Can I see?" she asked, excitement bubbling out of her.

I smiled. "Of course." I opened the container and revealed the cake to her.

"Oh my God, it's amazing!" she exclaimed.

"You think he'll like it?" I asked. I'd designed a cake of the Storm MC logo for Scott.

Her warm eyes found mine, and what I saw there gave me goosebumps. *Family*. She reached out and squeezed my hand. "There's nothing that you could do or make that Scott wouldn't love. My brother is completely in love with you."

Happiness flooded my body, but I was hesitant to accept it. "I don't think he's in love with me, Madison. It's only been a month."

She cocked her head. "Are you in love with him?"

I didn't even hesitate. "Yes."

Smiling again, she said, "So, if you can fall in love with him that quickly, it's highly possible that he can fall in love with you in that time too."

She made a good point.

"What's in the container?" J asked, coming into the kitchen.

Madison shushed him. "Harlow made Scott a birthday cake."

"Shit, what time's the party?" J asked.

"Why?" Madison asked, giving him that look that couples give each other when one of them believes the other has forgotten something or screwed something up.

"I have to pick up the steaks," he said.

"You forgot!" Madison accused him, playfully smacking him on the back.

He laughed. "Shit, you're a hard woman to please, Madison Cole. I just remembered, so technically I haven't forgotten because I'll have them in time for the party."

She laughed and pointed at the door. "Go! Hurry."

He leant in for a kiss and then he left, throwing a wink over his shoulder. I loved watching them together; there was so much love there and they had a lot of fun together.

"Oh crap, I forgot to tell J something. I'll be back in a minute," she promised as she ran out to find him.

I busied myself with getting plates and cups ready for the party. Scott was celebrating his thirty-fifth birthday and I'd been surprised when he agreed to this party. It had only been about two weeks since Bullet had tried to rape and kill me; two weeks since Scott and Blade had killed him. He'd been open with me about the fact that they'd taken care of him; he just hadn't told me how it had gone down. I didn't want to know, so I was glad he hadn't shared that much. Something told me that he never would; that it had actually been out of character for him to tell me as much as he had.

We'd invited some non club members to the party and I was excited. Mum and Cassie were coming and Lisa was too.

"Hey, babe," he murmured in my ear as he wrapped his arms around my waist.

I jumped; I'd been engrossed in my thoughts and hadn't heard him come in. "Hey, you."

He turned me around so I was facing him, his hands now resting on my ass. "I have a confession to tell you."

"What?"

"I overheard your conversation with Madison just now." He had a cheeky smile on his face.

"Did you? And what do you have to say about it?"

"Well, it reminded me of a conversation we started a couple of weeks ago, one where you asked me where I thought we were headed." He dipped his head and kissed me. When he broke the kiss, he asked, "You want to hear the answer to that?"

My heart expanded and I smiled; I loved it when Scott was happy like this. "Yes," I said, softly.

His eyes crinkled. I was done for, even without hearing his answer. Those crinkled eyes got to me every time. "This is headed to forever; forever on the back of my bike and forever in my bed."

My breathing slowed for a moment and then I whispered, "Forever."

He continued to smile. "Yeah, forever baby."

I reached up and touched his cheek, tracing the skin just under his eyes. "Crinkles," I said.

"What?" Confusion crossed his face.

"Crinkles. I love it when your eyes crinkle like that."

"I love you, sweetheart," he murmured, leaning in close for another kiss.

"I love you, too."

I'd never seen him coming; he'd worked his way into my life and my heart, and I knew that we would be forever. Scott didn't give his love easily, and I sensed that once you had it, you had it forever. And it was a fierce love; one that would hold strong through anything that life threw at us. Like I said, I'd never seen him coming and I sure as hell wasn't letting him go.

BONUS SCENE

CHRISTMAS WITH J & MADISON

THIS BONUS CHAPTER TAKES PLACE THE CHRISTMAS AFTER J AND MADISON GOT BACK TOGETHER IN STORM (J RETURNED TO THE CLUB IN THE SEPTEMBER OF THAT YEAR).

I opened my eyes and squinted as the sun that was streaming in through the window hit my face. Our bedroom was on the wrong side of the house for the sun, so on summer mornings the Queensland heat blazed with a scorching intensity. Personally, I loved the heat and didn't mind that my clothes were already starting to stick to me. Hell, it gave me a good reason to get them off and I knew that J would be down for that too.

From the view afforded me through the window it looked to be a glorious day outside and a smile snaked across my face; I loved Christmas in the sun which was where we would be spending today. I rolled over and snuggled up to J, gently laying a palm on his chest. It was early still, the bedside clock read only six thirty. Last night had been a late one; the club always spent Christmas Eve together and we hadn't gotten home until well after two am. It was a fantastic night, especially after such a shitty year.

"Mornin'," J murmured, and placed his hand on mine while his eyes sort mine.

"Merry Christmas, baby," I replied, and softly brushed my lips over his.

He grinned. "Fuck yeah. Where's my Christmas present?"

"We're exchanging them later, remember? At Scott's."

His smile was positively wicked now, and he slowly shook his head. "No, I'm talking about a private present, babe." He grasped my hand and moved it down his body, placing it on his cock. His eyes danced and he winked at me. "Let's see if you can do something with that."

I wrapped my hand around his hard cock and slowly slid it up and down his length.

"Best fucking present, babe," he muttered and then directed my lips to his.

Our kiss was unhurried yet full of passion, and desire curled through me. When J's fingers made their way to my clit, an explosion of pleasure hit me and I got so carried away that I bit his lip.

He pulled away from our kiss and grunted, "Shit -"

We were interrupted by my phone but J quickly rolled so that he was almost on top of me and attempted to block me from answering it. "Leave it. It's too fucking early for people to be ringing," he grumbled.

I pushed my palms against his chest in an effort to move him off me. "It might be important, J."

"Not fucking likely. It's probably just someone ringing to wish you a Merry Christmas, and that can wait," he said, as he resisted my efforts and tried to catch me in another kiss. I could feel his cock against my body and it almost distracted me from the ringing phone. Almost.

I gave him another forceful shove which succeeded in moving him enough so that I could slip underneath him and roll off the bed towards my phone. He recovered quickly and reached out to try and pull me back but it was futile as I'd already grabbed my phone and was about to answer it.

"Fucking cockblocker," he muttered as he got up and headed into the bathroom.

I ignored him and answered the phone call; it was Serena. "Hey, honey. Merry Christmas!" I said, excited to be hearing from her.

"Merry Christmas, chica!"

A huge grin was now plastered across my face. "I miss you," I said, and it was the absolute truth. Serena and I hadn't seen each other for a couple of months and I was having serious withdrawals.

"Well, put the kettle on and open the bloody door and let me in."

"What?" I screamed, "You're here?" I ran to the front door and threw it open. I was greeted with the sight of Serena and Blake.

Blake stepped forward and caught me in a hug. As he pulled away, he murmured, "It's been too long, baby girl."

I smiled at him and nodded. "It really has." We hadn't seen each other since August, just before J returned from the road trip my father had banished him on. I'd spent some time in Coffs Harbour while J was away but we hadn't made the time to catch up since then.

"You're looking well. Much better than the last time I saw you," he said, approvingly. "I hate to admit it but J must be good for you."

I sighed. Blake and J hadn't had the opportunity to get to know each other yet and Blake still held reservations about my relationship. "Yes, honey, J is good for me. You'll see."

Serena pushed Blake out of the way and threw herself at me. "I've fucking missed you! Why can't you and biker boy move to Coffs?"

I laughed. "You could move to Brisbane."

She let me go but held onto my shoulders and

looked me in the eyes. "You'll never move back will you?" she asked, with a more serious tone.

I shook my head. "I don't think so. We're pretty settled here."

"And once he gets that ring on your finger, that'll be it I guess," she mused.

"She's got a ring on her finger," J said, as he came up behind me and wrapped his arms around my waist. His lips brushed my cheek in a kiss.

Serena winked at me before saying to him, "That's not the ring I'm talking about, J. Engagement rings are pretty and all, but you need to hurry up and get that wedding ring on there."

He grunted, and said, "I'm not the one holding the fucking process up, sweetheart." His frustration was clear for the world to see. "You need to talk to your girl here; talk some sense into her."

"It's happening. We're just having some trouble booking the venue that we want. Aren't we, baby?" I turned and looked at J for him to verify what I'd said.

He shook his head. "No, *we're* not. I'd marry you in our backyard. Today."

I sighed. "I know, and as far as I'm concerned, we're as good as married. But you know I've always wanted my wedding reception to be on the river so we just have to wait for the date they have free."

"When is that?" Blake chimed in.

"Not until February next year," J muttered, and

turned to head into the kitchen. "That's enough wedding talk. Who wants coffee?"

Serena arched an eyebrow at me. "All's not well with you two?" she asked softly.

I linked my arm through hers and smiled. "Actually, all is pretty bloody good with us. He's just sulking because he can't get his way on this and you know how bossy he can be. It'll do him good to compromise for once."

"Absolutely," she agreed.

We followed J into the kitchen with Blake close behind. As we were walking I could see her taking in the house; checking everything out. Neither of them had ever visited us here and I knew they were keen to see where I lived now and to make sure I was doing okay living with J.

"Nice place," Serena finally commented.

"Different to what you thought?" I asked, noting her surprise.

"Very. Have you changed it a lot since you moved in?"

I surveyed the room. When I'd moved in, his house had been just that; a house. He hadn't decorated it at all. I'd slowly started adding my own touch to it. J hadn't minded, although he'd drawn the line at adding a cream couch and multi-coloured cushions to the living room. He'd told me that he didn't want a fucking rainbow in there, so we'd agreed on a black leather sofa that looked great with the white and grey walls. After we'd finished with the living room, J decided that he quite liked the added colour so we'd painted some feature walls throughout. We had a red and black colour scheme in our bedroom, charcoal grey and black in the bathroom and turquoise in the kitchen. He wasn't so fussed on the turquoise but it was my favourite colour so he'd relented and agreed to whatever I wanted for that space. The running joke in the club revolved around J's decorating skills; the boys were constantly giving him shit about how stylish our home was.

"Yeah, we've painted the whole house and I've added rugs and paintings, stuff like that. And I think I've finally convinced J to do some work on the yard, maybe add a pool," I replied.

"Well, I love what you guys have done," Serena said, "And I'm in love with that huge ass TV you've got."

I rolled my eyes. "Bloody men and their toys! It takes up so much room but J insisted he have it. Oh, and he also had to have an X-box. He and Scott love that fucking thing."

Serena laughed and Blake muttered from behind us, "Looks like he has some redeeming qualities." I ignored him and wondered how long it would take for him and J to get over their issues with each other.

We entered the kitchen to find J working the Nespresso machine; another of my home improvements. I took a minute to enjoy the view of my man working in the kitchen wearing only a pair of jeans. It was a view I would never get tired of. J was over six foot of solid muscle; his back, chest and arms inked with numerous tattoos including the club tattoo on his back that was in full view at the moment. Watching his muscles flex while he reached for mugs shot heat through my body and I stood transfixed, admiring him.

Serena slapped me on the arm. "Earth to Maddy. You want me to pick your tongue up off the floor, chica?"

She was grinning at me and I laughed. "Yeah, I might need it for later," I joked, winking at J as he caught my eye.

He nodded and smirked, "That tongue is multi-fucking-talented. We'll definitely need it for later on."

J and his dirty mouth. Serena broke out in laughter. "I'd forgotten that you had a way with words, J," she said.

"I have a way with other things too, sweetheart. Just ask Madison."

"Okay, enough, you two," I said, noting Blake's reaction to this conversation. He didn't look like he was enjoying it and the last thing I wanted was for him to be uncomfortable in my home.

I sat next to him at the kitchen table. "I'm so happy to see you," I said softly to him as Serena and J made coffee together and continued on with their banter.

His smile reached his eyes. "Me too. And it's good to see where you're living now."

I read between the lines. "He's good for me, Blake. I haven't felt this happy and at peace for a long time."

He nodded slowly, like he didn't quite believe me. Blake wasn't the kind of person to make quick judgments; he would need to observe for himself and make up his own mind over time. "You certainly do seem happier and less angry. But I'm not entirely convinced, baby girl. I don't want you to get hurt again so just let me see for myself okay. I need to know you're going to be alright because you were fucking broken the last time he hurt you."

It was a good thing we were a little way away from where J was because if he heard what Blake had just said he wouldn't take too kindly to it. I reached out and squeezed Blake's hand. "I get it. And you will see, I promise." We sat in silence for a moment as we both processed what the other had said. Our friendship was deep and I knew that he was only doing what a good friend would do. His concern touched my heart; I felt blessed to have a friend that cared that much.

"How long are you and Serena staying for?" I finally asked.

"It's just a flying visit this time. I need to get back to the restaurant for tomorrow night so we'll be leaving early tomorrow morning." His disappointment was evident.

"We really need to make more of an effort next year, don't we?" I reflected. Since I'd moved back to Brisbane time had gotten away from me and I knew that

Blake was really busy with his business too. But friends and family had to come first and I needed the reminder.

He nodded in agreement. "Yeah, we do."

We were interrupted by Serena who placed coffees in front of us. "I made yours with the strongest pod, Blake. Figured you'd need it after the small amount of sleep you've had," she said.

J brought the rest of the coffees over and sat next to me. "What time did you leave this morning?" he asked Blake.

Blake met J's eyes. "Just after two am," he answered him, and then looked to Serena, "Thanks for the coffee. I do need it, babe."

Well, this was a civilised conversation and it warmed me to see J and Blake conversing like this. I just hoped it would continue.

We drank our coffees and caught up a little before Serena asked, "So, what's the plan for today?"

I broke out in a huge smile because I had been looking forward to today for weeks. Christmas was one of my favourite times of the year and I'd been planning our get together for a long time. I ran my hand over J's arm excitedly and he chuckled as we made eye contact. He'd put up with my plotting and planning but I think I'd nearly driven him insane this last week with my mad frenzy to get everything finalised.

"What hasn't she got planned, more to the point," J murmured.

"Oh, hush," I said, as I leaned over and planted a kiss on his lips, still grinning like a mad woman.

"Madison is like a woman possessed at Christmas time," Blake commented, obviously remembering my crazy demands on my friends at this time of year.

"Tell me about it," J said, " She's been shopping, cooking and hanging shit for weeks, and I'm not only talking about in this house. You should see Scott's house. That poor fucker never saw her coming. He arrived home one night and it was like Santa had purged his fucking warehouse in there."

Blake almost choked on his coffee as he started laughing. "Fuck, Madison, you could have come and decorated my restaurant."

J saw my eyes light up at the thought of that job. "Jesus, don't fucking get her started."

I slapped him playfully on the arm. "Don't be mean! You secretly love it. I can tell."

He grinned at me and snaked an arm around my waist, pulling me close so that our lips brushed. "Baby, I love that you love it. And watching you get up that ladder to hang the fucking tinsel…yeah, I love that and that's no secret."

"Anyway, moving along," I suggested, because otherwise I could see J and Blake making fun of me for awhile, "We're spending the day at Scott's house because he has a pool. Mum and Dad, and some of the boys from the club will be there. It'll be lunch and then kicking back with a drink for the afternoon."

"Sounds great, honey," Serena said, "Are any of these biker boys hot?"

Now it was J's turn to almost choke. "I wouldn't let any of those guys near you so don't even go there." His protective streak surprised the shit out of me but at the same time I was really happy about it because it told me that Serena meant something to him.

"Pfft," Serena waved her hand at him, "I think I can look out for myself, J. And besides, I'm not looking for a long term thing, just a bit of fun."

J pushed his chair back and stood up. "Is there ever such a thing as a bit of fun for a chick?" he asked her.

"You don't know me very well. I'm always up for a bit of fun. Don't need the hassle that a full time man brings."

J raised his eyebrows, clearly not convinced. "Yeah, well just remember what I've said."

I stood and took over the conversation; I was fairly certain that Serena and J would never come to an understanding about this. She really did just want a bit of fun but I knew that in J's experience, women said that but never meant it. "We're heading over to Scott's at about ten thirty. I need to have a shower now and then J needs to give me my present," I said, grinning at him. He looked a little stressed; the present buying hadn't been without its issues. I couldn't understand why men seemed to struggle so much with this.

He smacked me on the ass. "I'll give you your present but not until you give me mine. And I'm talking about the one that you almost gave me this morning, babe."

"Promises, promises," I teased him, and then turned to Blake and Serena, "Make yourselves at home. Blake, feel free to play with the X-box. We'll be back." And with that, I dragged J towards the bedroom.

A minute or so later, he shut the bedroom door behind us and then pulled me to him, wrapping his arms around me and gripping my ass. He bent his head down to mine and caught my lips in a kiss. It was a deep kiss and he consumed me, body and soul. I would always be lost to this man; anything he wanted from me, he could have. I wouldn't be able to deny him.

He ended our kiss but didn't pull his face away from mine. His lips remained close to mine and when he spoke, warm breath hit me and sent a jolt of pleasure straight through me. "Feels so fucking good," he growled, and squeezed my ass before letting his hands roam over my body, up to my hips and then my breasts before trailing them down to the bottom of the t-shirt I was wearing. It was his t-shirt and he removed it in one quick movement, and threw it on the floor.

His eyes slid over my naked body and I felt them everywhere; felt the desire they traced as he took his sweet time looking at me. J never seemed to tire of this and I reveled in it; I loved that he got so much pleasure out of simply watching me.

I reached out and slowly unzipped his jeans. When my hands lightly brushed over his skin he sucked in a breath. After I had his zip undone, I pulled his jeans down and he stepped out of them, kicking them to the side, out of our way. I moved closer to him so that we were skin to skin, and took his cock in my hand and stroked him. His hands moved over my ass and he dropped his head onto my shoulder as I continued to pleasure him. I could hear his ragged breathing and feel his body begin to jerk as his cock grew even harder.

"Fuck. Won't be long," he muttered and lifted his head, our eyes meeting.

"Merry Christmas, baby," I whispered, keeping the momentum going with his cock.

Suddenly, he moved my hand away from him and lifted me up so that my legs wrapped around him. He walked me to the bed and deposited me on it. "I need to be in you," he rasped, and moved over me on the bed.

I pulled his lips to mine in a frenzied kiss as my arms went around him. One of his hands moved over my breasts and then moved down my body until it found my clit, circling it and driving me wild. I dug my fingernails into his back and he grunted in pleasure. "J, I need your cock now," I begged, and he didn't waste any time. As he entered me, I lifted my hips to him and wrapped my legs around him. He thrust hard and fast, and it felt so fucking good. I swore his cock was made for me.

We lost ourselves as he kept up his unrelenting pace and fucked me with abandon. He worked me into a state of fevered passion, my entire body lit with the electric sensations that only J had ever been able to evoke in me. Our bodies were a wild mess of sweat and desire as we worked our way towards bliss.

"Fucking love you," he grunted, as he thrust in as far as he could. J's sweet talk during sex always affected me and a thrill shot through me at his words. It hit me right in my core. I closed my eyes and white lights flashed as an orgasm took hold. My legs squeezed tighter around him and I clenched my pussy around his cock; the pleasure almost at a peak. He stilled for a moment and then his cock jerked as he found his release and we came together.

J lay still on top of me for a couple of moments afterwards and then he lifted his head and smiled at me, dusting a kiss over my lips. "Best fucking Christmas present."

"Yeah, it was," I agreed and we lay like that for another moment or so, eyes and bodies locked together, enjoying the closeness.

He eventually rolled off me, onto his back.

I got up off the bed and headed into the bathroom to have a shower. Reaching into the shower I turned on the taps, letting the hot water filter through before I turned on the cold tap. Even though it was summer, I still had to have a warm shower which J found ridiculous. He couldn't understand why I didn't have cold showers in summer. Lost in my thoughts, I didn't hear him enter the room so he startled me when he said, "Best fucking Christmas too, babe."

I almost jumped out of my skin. "Bloody hell, you scared the shit out of me," I grumbled, but when I turned to face him, all annoyance left me as I was treated to a view of him naked, with his arms stretched above his head, hands gripping onto the doorframe. "Yeah, baby, best Christmas ever," I softened, and laid a smile on him.

He dropped his arms and came towards me. When he stepped into my personal space, he lifted his hand and caressed my cheek gently. "So fucking thankful to have you back. Never letting you go again. Okay?"

He phrased it like a question but I knew J and so I knew it wasn't a question. But yet, I reassured him. "I'm not going anywhere, J. You're stuck with me."

My words must have been the exact right words because he roughly pulled me to him, our bodies almost slapping together. He dipped his head and grazed my ear lightly with his lips. "Good," he murmured, and then kissed me with a passion that wiped all coherent thought from my mind.

When he finished and pulled away, he slapped me on the ass yet again, and muttered, "Now, let's get today over with so that we can come back here and you can give me another Christmas present."

BONUS SCENE

VALENTINE'S DAY WITH J & MADISON

*THIS BONUS CHAPTER TAKES PLACE IN THE FEBRUARY
AFTER THE CHRISTMAS CHAPTER.*

Warm breath tickled my neck and strong arms enveloped me from behind. I leant back into him and placed my hands on his arms. This was my safe place, and being with him like this drowned out the noise from the party that was in full swing around us.

His lips brushed my neck and he murmured, "You're driving me fucking insane in that dress, baby. I need it off you and I need that soon. How much longer do you want to stick around here?"

We were at the Anti Valentine's party at Scott's house that Harlow had organised, and had been here for more than four hours now so I figured we could split anytime soon. She wouldn't be upset; nothing much fazed her and it was one of the reasons why I loved her so much. Actually, Harlow was the best thing that had ever happened to my brother so I loved her unconditionally for that alone.

I decided to play with J a little though. "We can't leave yet, we haven't been here long enough."

He groaned in my ear and then moved his hand to cover my breast, fingers circling my nipple. It was a good thing we were in a dark corner where nobody could see what he was doing. J wouldn't care either way; he'd fuck me wherever and whenever he could, but I preferred privacy. "I don't give a fuck how long we haven't been here. In ten minutes I'm taking you home so I can rip that fucking dress off you and taste your sweet pussy, so I'd suggest you say your goodbyes now. We clear?"

Heat sizzled throughout me; this was the side of J I loved the most. His dirty mouth and bossy ways never failed to turn me on. He moved his hand off my breast but I quickly stopped him and directed it back there. "For the next five minutes I want your hands on me, J, and I want you to imagine tasting me and fucking me. Then I'll go and say goodbye and then you can take me home and rip my dress off. Oh, and by the way, you'll be buying me a new one. Are we clear?"

He growled, and gripped my breast harder. "Fuck. If you're not careful I'll be ripping this dress off here." His other hand came up to my other breast and he roughly kneaded both of them. Lust for him took over both my mind and body, and I leant my head back on his shoulder and softly moaned with pleasure. His erection pressed firmly into me and I reached around behind me to stroke him. When my hand found him, his body jerked and he pulled away from me, dropping both hands from my breast and catching my hand in his. "Fuck ten minutes, babe, we're going now."

As he started to stalk towards the front door, I pulled on his hand to slow him down. "J, I need to say goodbye, at least to Harlow and Scott."

He contemplated that for a second, and then replied, "Fine. But make it quick, Madison. No fucking about because my dick can't take much more. I need to be inside you."

I pulled his face down to mine and kissed him. "I need that too," I said softly as I ended the kiss.

His hand wrapped around my neck and he drew me closer to him so that our faces were only a breath apart. Our eyes locked and his searched mine for a moment. "Valentine's Day is a load of fucking shit as far as I'm concerned but for some reason it's making me want to tell you how much I love you, baby. And even though we're not married yet, you're mine for fucking ever, even if this bloody wedding doesn't go ahead."

Smiling at his possessiveness, I said, "J, this wedding is going ahead. I know it feels like everything has been against it happening but trust me, it's happening. In less than two weeks I will be your wife, and you'll be stuck with me forever."

"Thank Christ for that," he muttered, and then a deadly serious look came across his face as he added, "I hope you know that I will never let you go. Even if shit gets bad, I'm not letting you go. I will fucking kill anything or anyone that comes between us if I have to. And if you ever think about walking away, you'll have a fucking fight on your hands, babe."

I pushed myself into him and pressed my lips to his, tasting him. The sensations that his words caused in my body were amazing; he had the power to set me alight with desire from his words alone. "That's why I love you, J. That you would fight for me, that you won't let me go... that's all I need. I don't need roses or chocolates on Valentine's Day to know how much you love me."

"Good. Now, find Harlow and Scott so we can get out of here."

Doing what he said, I found Harlow a couple of minutes later in the kitchen. Of course she was in the kitchen; this girl could cook up a storm and every man in the club was in heaven whenever she visited the clubhouse with her food.

She saw me and her face lit up. We hadn't had much time to catch up tonight and I knew she'd be a little disappointed that we were leaving now but she'd understand. "We're going to head out now, honey," I said.

She took one look at J and nodded. His intent to get me home must have been evident, and everyone knew not to mess with J. Especially where I was concerned. "Thanks for coming," she said as she hugged me goodbye. "Even though I dislike Valentine's Day, I've got to say that I'm looking forward to the after party and it looks like you and J are too," she whispered in my ear before letting me go. Her eyes were twinkling and she laid a huge smile on me.

I laughed and held up my hand in a defensive type gesture. "I've told you before, I don't want to hear the words sex and Scott in the same sentence, so don't go there. I don't need to know those things about my brother."

Scott wandered into the kitchen at that moment, catching only my last sentence. "What things don't you need to know about me?" he asked as he stood behind Harlow and put his arm around her shoulders. I watched as she sunk back into him, a content look crossing her face.

"I don't need to know about your after party activities."

He smirked. "No, you definitely don't need to know about that. Nobody needs to know what I've got planned for Harlow tonight."

I held up both hands now. "J and I are leaving now; before you say anymore. Thanks for a great party."

J was laughing by now. "Thanks, brother. I should

have got you to start talking sooner. Would have gotten Madison home a lot earlier if I had."

I smacked him on the chest and glared at him. "Don't encourage him. Seriously, you two are wicked together."

"You're forgetting one thing, Madison. I don't share Harlow with anyone and that means my lips are sealed. What Harlow and I do at our private parties is between just the two of us so you never need to worry that you're going to hear about it because that's never going to fucking happen."

"Thank goodness for that," I replied. I couldn't tell you why, but even though I loved sex and wasn't a prude in any way, I didn't want to know about my brother's sex life.

J slapped my ass. "Time to go, babe," he said before leaning down to whisper in my ear, "I've got a dress to rip off."

Scott let Harlow go and we hugged goodbye while J and Scott said goodbye. Then he led me outside to his Jeep. He'd had to drive that tonight rather than his bike due to what I was wearing. Opening the door for me, he stood back and watched me, a small smile playing on his lips.

"What are you smiling at?"

"I'm just enjoying the show, babe. Watching you in that dress is pure fucking heaven."

Leaning forward, I murmured, "It's a shame you

didn't realise that all night I've had nothing on underneath it then, isn't it?"

I watched as he took this in; playing with J like this was one of my favourite things to do. "Jesus fucking Christ, woman. Get in the damn car now."

Smiling, I said, "Happy Valentine's Day, J." And then I did what I'd been told.

For more bonus scenes, visit www.ninalevinebooks.com

ALSO BY NINA LEVINE

ABOUT THE AUTHOR

Nina Levine

Dreamer.
Coffee Lover.
Gypsy at heart.

USA Today Bestselling author who writes about alpha men & the women they love.

When I'm not creating with words you will find me planning my next getaway, visiting somewhere new in the world, having a long conversation over coffee and cake with a friend, creating with paper or curled up with a good book and chocolate.

I've been writing since I was twelve. Weaving words together has always been a form of therapy for me especially during my harder times. These days I'm proud that my words help others just as much as they help me.

ACKNOWLEDGMENTS

So many people have helped me get this book finished and released. As I continue on my publishing journey, I am blown away daily by the kindness of so many people.

Firstly, my family & friends. Without your understanding and encouragement, none of this would be possible. Especially my daughter - love you, baby.

I'd like to say a huge thank you to K, my beta reader. You especially came through for me at the eleventh hour and threw out some great ideas - love you!

To Levine's Ladies! OMG, you girls ROCK! Seriously. I love the shit out of you all and love dropping in daily to chat with you. Apart from helping me spread the word about my books, you provide amazing support and encouragement to me every bloody day.

And that #DAILYFIX ??? LOVE IT!

To my readers. WOW!! Some days I am speechless when I get a beautiful message of support or encouragement or just a thanks for writing my book. You may never know how much a message means to me. And those reviews you have taken the time to write? From the bottom of my heart - THANK YOU!

To the authors and bloggers who support, encourage and help promote me - thank you so much! I'm not going to name names except for one - mainly because there are so many and I don't want to accidentally forget anyone and offend you. But if you have ever shared my links or even just chatted with me, please know that my gratitude is endless.

Jani Kay. You are amazing, sexy lady. I love chatting with you - we are so alike in many ways and you just get me. Your support has blown me away! Thank you, thank you, thank you!

www.ninalevinebooks.com

53289388R00163

Made in the USA
Columbia, SC
15 March 2019